**NAVEEN** is a renowned novelist and short story writer in Telugu. He has 23 published novels and more than 50 short stories to his credit. He is the pioneer of the stream of consciousness narrative technique in Telugu. His first novel and indubitable masterpiece, *Ampasayya* (Bed of Arrows), besides going through five editions, has been translated into Hindi and Tamil. His *Mauna Ragalu* (Silent Tunes) and *Karuna* (named after the heroine) have been translated into Kannada. Some of his other highly acclaimed novels are: *Mullapodalu* (Thorn Bushes), *Anthasravanti* (Inner Stream), *Cheekati Rojulu* (Dark Days), *Vichalita* (The Disturbed Woman) *Women's College* and *Sankellu* (Chains). The last of these has been made into a TV serial.

Naveen's short stories stand comparison with the best short fiction anywhere in the world. So far two collections of them, *Life in a College* and *Enimido Adugu* (Eighth Step), have appeared. Apart from winning prizes many of them have also been translated into Hindi, English, Tamil and Kannada.

Naveen has received many honours and awards for his contribution to the Telugu fiction. Special mention may be made of AP Sahitya Akademi (Telugu University) Award for the best novel (*Anthasravanti*) in 1994 and the Ministry of Human Resource Development's Senior Fellowship in Literature in 1997.

Naveen has been the Principal of an undergraduate college in the AP Education Service. He is currently working on a research-based novel as part of the Senior Fellowship mentioned above.

# LIFESCAPES
## TELUGU SHORT STORIES

**NAVEEN**

**ATLANTIC PUBLISHERS AND DISTRIBUTORS**

*Published by*
**ATLANTIC PUBLISHERS AND DISTRIBUTORS**
B-2, Vishal Enclave, Opp. Rajouri Garden,
New Delhi-110 027
Phones : 5413460, 5429987

*Sales Office*
4215/1, Ansari Road, Darya Ganj,
New Delhi-110 002
Phones : 3273880, 3285873, 3280451
Fax : 91-11-3285873
e-mail : gupta.atlantc@axcess.net.in
web site : http://www.atlanticbooks.com



*Typeset at*
APD Computer Graphics, Delhi

*Printed in India at*
Mehra Offset Press, Delhi

# PREFACE

Naveen enjoys immense popularity among the Telugu readers. He has boldly treated many new themes and introduced a number of new narrative techniques in the Telugu fiction. A clear intellectual edge and minute analysis of the human psyche are the two great strengths of his fiction. His keen perception and deep probing into the issues facing the contemporary society lend his works a seriousness which is rarely found elsewhere. Reading Naveen is at once an aesthetic as well as intellectual experience.

Naveen's short stories encompass a wide spectrum of life. They reveal his insights into the intricacies of the psychological, social and political life of the Telugu people and lay bare the reality behind the manifest. The themes touched upon by him in this collection of short stories are therefore naturally as varied as the psychological conflicts experienced by the sensitive among us, exploitation of children and adolescents by unfeeling guardians and employers, violence in rural Telangana, the subhuman lives of beggars and subalterns, the ill-treatment regularly meted out to women within and outside marriage and the insensitivity of women themselves to the genuine needs of their men. That is indeed a mouthful of life to savour and mull over.

It has been my long felt wish to present these captivating and thought provoking short stories in English translation, a task which I have not been able to shoulder all by myself. Fortunately for me, some of the best, indeed the very cream, of the translators we have in Andhra Pradesh, have readily come forward to share the responsibility with me. I am grateful to every one of them.

The choice of the stories is wholly the author's. A careful look at them will reveal that they present life as it obtains in Andhra Pradesh today without ideologically colouring it and without straining to be politically correct.

I am aware of the conflicting theories governing fidelity in translation. My guiding principle however has been "readability in English without sacrificing the spirit of the source text." Where no violence is done to the source text and subject to the approval of the author, certain liberties have been taken by most of the translators, all in the interest of readability in English. Now it is for the enlightened readers to judge whether what my fellow translators, and that includes the author himself, and I have done is right or not so right.

**M.R.**
*Editor*

# CONTENTS

# MANORAMA

When I came to know that I had been appointed as junior lecturer at Hanamkonda, I felt very happy. I boarded train at Secunderabad at six in the morning and reached Kazipet at half past eight.

As I waited for the city bus to take me to Hanamkonda, an Ambassador car pulled up beside me. The man at the steering wheel appeared to be familiar to me, but I could not recall his name immediately.

He saw me and said, smiling broadly, 'Hey mama, after such a long time! How are you?'

I recognized him now. 'Orey Mohan, it's you? I couldn't recognize you at once,' I said excitedly.

'That's how it's bound to be! Would you remember country bumpkins like me,' Mohan said sarcastically. 'How are things? How has it happened that you are here?'

'From now on I will be living in your town. I got a job in a junior college. I am going there to join duty today,' I explained.

'What a great news, mama! I'm dying for a friend like you. I can't believe that after such a long time we got another chance to be together. I too am going that way... come...sit,' Mohan said, opening the door.

I got into the car and sat beside Mohan. He started the car and put it into gear.

'When did you buy this car?' I asked.

'Do you think I bought it to go for pleasure rides? I bought it to make a living. A bank gave me loan under the Self-employment Scheme. I'm using it as a taxi.'

'So, that's it. I've been wondering when you have become so rich as to buy a car. That's okay. How are you? How is life?'

'Hell of a life, mama! It's terrible. A desert is better than this life.'

'What's this Mohan? You used to laugh and make others laugh all the time. We still remember your jokes. Not even twenty five years of age, how come you are disillusioned so very much with life?'

'If I have ever been happy since birth, it was when we were studying at college.'

'You should have taken studies a little more seriously. You could have got a good job. You neglected studies, moving with people all the time. Your not passing B.A. along with us...'

Before I could finish my sentence Mohan said, 'Not every one can study well. I managed to graduate from high school by cheating in the examination, because cheating was possible. At the junior college, it was a little strict. I failed twice, but somehow completed Intermediate. I never imagined they would conduct examinations so very strictly at the degree college.'

'Have you appeared for the subjects you failed in the B.A. examination again?'

'Unless I passed B.A., how do you think the bank had given me a loan?' Mohan looked at a beautiful girl crossing the road and whistled. He pointed her out to me and said, 'Look at her, a beauty, isn't she?'

'So you haven't got rid of your habit of losing your mind on looking at girls! By the by, Mohan, have you got married?'

'Indeed I got married, but not for myself.'

'Then, for whom?'

'You ask that question as if you don't know anything about such things. In our country, have you ever seen any boy or girl marrying for his or her own sake? In the films, they never marry except when they are in love. But in real life, can you show me anybody who has married like that?'

'In real life too there are people who fall in love and marry only then.'

'I used to think like that all these years. If at all I married, I wanted the girl to be the one I had been in love with....But what has happened? My people chose a girl from a family of my relatives and forcibly *tied* her to me.'

'Leave it Mohan. Life is never as sweet as we dream of it. We have to adjust.'

'Adjust! One day? Two days? Who is prepared to adjust life long?' Mohan got very angry. The severity and impatience in his words surprised me. We had already reached the college. 'That's okay. Forget about me. Are you married Raghu?' Mohan asked me bringing the car to a halt in front of the college gate.

I opened the door and said, getting out, 'Not yet.'

'Okay mama. At least you should love a girl and get married to her.'

I smiled but made no answer.

'Where will you go after the college?' Mohan enquired.

'I've got to stay here till four in the evening. Then I'll try for a room somewhere near here.'

'Oh, don't you worry about a room. My house is big enough. You can stay with me for some days.'

'No, Mohan. There will be bachelors like me working at this college. I'll move in with one of them.'

'I'm no better than a bachelor myself. Don't think I'm greatly enjoying married life. Give me a chance to spend a few days with you. I'll be back here at four. Wait for me,' Mohan said and drove off.

I walked towards the principal's office still thinking of Mohan.

✡ ✡ ✡

Mohan was my classmate at college. We were studying in Hyderabad. We used to live in neighbouring houses and it didn't take much time for us to make friends. Mohan had the habit of addressing all his acquaintances and friends as mama, which literally means 'uncle.' I hated to be addressed as 'mama' by him in the beginning. With the passage of time, like everybody else, I was also influenced by Mohan's charming innocence and stopped worrying about what he called me.

With his good nature, specially with his open-heartedness, Mohan used to easily attract people to him. They used to be greatly pleased and amused at these qualities in him.

Mohan used to keenly watch girls all the time. He used to do little things for them, even when they didn't ask him to do so. After the classes, when they were preparing to go home, he used to fetch rickshaws for them. When rickshaws were not available anywhere near, he used to walk great distances to fetch one. He used to go and see for himself whether the girls reached their homes safely or not. Whenever they lost anything — purse, handkerchief, change or notebook — he used to somehow find them and safely return to them. Whenever rowdies tried to tease these girls, he was there to save the situation by requesting, and even begging the rowdies not to harm them.

Mohan was extremely good-looking. With a height of five feet and ten inches, fair skin, black curly hair, clear, black and large eyes, broad forehead, roundish face and neatly trimmed moustache, Mohan would make a permanent impress on anyone at the very first sight. He used to spend a lot of time looking at himself in the mirror. He was always in spotless white clothes, which shone brightly in the sun.

Mohan was a movie buff. He specially liked the scenes in which the hero came to rescue the heroine. He would clap excitedly whenever such scenes came on the screen.

One endearing quality in Mohan was his sense of humour. No matter how many jokes we made about him, he was never offended. On the other hand, he used to join us in laughing at himself.

While still at college, Mohan had once even fallen in love. He said, he was in love with Rama who was the most beautiful of our class girls. He dreamt of her day and night. He persuaded me for many days to draft a love letter for him. I asked him to make sure that there was clear evidence of Rama being in love with him and warned him that he would land himself in difficulty otherwise. It seems, she smiled at him once and on the basis of that he jumped to the conclusion that she was in love with him. For months on end, he expected that she herself would write a love letter to him, but Rama left the college in the middle nobody knew why.

During those days, Mohan was fond of saying that he would go in for a love marriage and never agree to an arranged marriage. Now it was painful for me to learn that he had been forced into an arranged marriage by his elders.

✡ ✡ ✡

That evening Mohan took me to his house in his car. He said he owned the house. It was a big but old house. He inherited it from his mother's family. There were six rooms in all. I was given one room.

'Where is your wife?' I asked, finding none in that big house.

'She has been to her parents' place. It's because she is not here that the house is peaceful. To tell you the truth, I'm happy only when she is away.'

'I understand that you prefer the life of a bachelor, even when you are married.'

'What a marriage!' Mohan threw up his hands. 'Is that a marriage? It's like forcing poison down your throat... chi, chi!'

I felt I should drop the topic there. We remained silent for a while. Later, we went out to a hotel to have dinner. Back home, we talked about our college days, late into the night.

One thing appeared very clearly to me in every word of Mohan: he was not getting any pleasure from married life. It may be because of this that he fell a victim of extreme discontentment in life. He was still hoping that something great would happen and that his life would take a great turn for the better.

About fifteen days after I moved into the house, Mohan's wife came from the village. Aruna was by no means a beautiful woman. She was not ugly either. But for the handsome and sensitive Mohan, she was certainly no match. Her manners were unrefined and her behaviour was coarse. Her words, her movements and her dress — in all these, her coarseness made itself apparent.

On the day she came Mohan returned home very late. I knew him to drink, but that night he seemed to have helped himself liberally to drink. As soon as he entered the house he shouted, 'Eey devil, have you already come? Perhaps you thought I'm having a great time here all by myself. Your father surely has lots of money, hasn't he? Couldn't he have fed you for a few more days?'

'If you didn't like me, why have you married me?' Aruna confronted him with her argument.

'I haven't married you, you log of a woman. Your father and my father ganged up to tie you to me.'

'You were not a child at that time. Why didn't you tell them that you didn't like to marry me? Oh, what shall I do now?'

'Go and jump into the Ganga or the Godavari, but don't come to my house again. Don't cross my path. I'll send you monthly maintenance as some kind of moral responsibility on my part, if you want.'

'What kind of justice is this, nayano ....?' Aruna began to shout and wail.

'Why are you crying, you slut? Shut up.... Do you want the neighbours to think that I'm beating my wife after getting drunk? Will you shut up or shall I really kick the hell out of you?'

'You want to kick me? Then, kick. I want to see how you will kick me,' Aruna said defiantly.

I thought the situation was getting out of hand. I went out of the house and asked Mohan to follow me. Mohan came out, hugged me and said, 'Look at this mama! Look, what has become of my life?' He started crying like a child. That night he slept in my room.

Next morning, I took him for a walk and for a long time tried to explain to him why he should adjust, since he was married to her and nothing could be done about it now. I said, 'You should forget your adolescent dreams. There is a big difference between dreams and reality. It surprises me that, at your age too, you haven't learnt to accept the realities of life. If you still think somebody would come into your life, somebody would love you and that your dreams will come true, I'm afraid, it's your foolishness. It's equally foolish to lose what you have in the hope of something terrific happening to you.' I spoke with him in this vein for a long time. Still, there was no change in Mohan. As long as Aruna stayed, he drank heavily and came home very late in the night. He would then quarrel with her, come to my room and sleep there. After a week or so, Aruna went back to her parents' place.

After she left I confronted him with a point blank question, 'What do you propose to do now?'

'I'm going to divorce her,' Mohan replied equally directly.

'You are a fool. You may see better days if you are nice to Aruna. Who knows, she may change,' I counselled.

'Who? That devil? You think she will change!' Mohan said in great surprise and walked away.

After Aruna had gone away, Mohan was his usual self once again. He stopped drinking and resumed his pleasantries with me.

✡ ✡ ✡

More than a month after I moved to Hanamkonda, one evening, Mohan appeared to be in high spirits. As soon as he came home, he barged into my room and said, 'You know what happened today, mama? I saw the girl whom I've been searching all my life.'

'Which girl are you talking about?'

'The girl whom I'm going to love — I was returning from Mamnoor. I saw her near Ashoka Talkies. A stunning beauty! Never saw one like her even in dreams. When she saw me, she smiled and waved her hand to me. I went a little farther, parked my car by the side of the road and looked back. She was gone!'

'Where had she disappeared so suddenly?'

'That's what I don't understand. I thought she entered one of the shops there. I searched every shop, but couldn't find her.'

'It's all your illusion. Stop being foolish.'

'It's not at all an illusion. I've seen her with my own two eyes. She looked at me and smiled. She waved her hand as if she was calling me. I swear. Believe me.'

'She must have smiled at somebody she knew or she must have been a mad woman or a prostitute.'

'Shut up! If you speak like that I'll kick you,' Mohan held my collar and almost knocked me down. It was the first time he was so angry with me.

For a whole week after that, Mohan didn't speak to me. However, I kept myself informed of what he was doing during this week. He would go to Ashoka Talkies everyday and search all the shops for his dream girl. But she was not to be seen anywhere.

He came to me at the end of the week and said excitedly, 'I've seen her today at the bus-stand... from very near... but, by the time I parked the car and came back, she boarded the Hyderabad-bound bus and had gone away.'

'Ayyo, how sad!' I said pretending to be serious.

'If I were one minute early, I could have met her.' He was immune to the mockery in my tone.

'Did she smile at you this time too?'

'Yes, just like last time.... She smiled the moment she saw me and waved her hand.'

I laughed.

'I know, you don't believe me. I swear on my favourite god, Yadagiri Narasimha Swamy. I've really seen her. She really waved her hand to call me to her.' Mohan put his right hand on his head for emphasis.

'If she really waved her hand, why was that she gave you the slip?'

'Can't you understand a simple thing like that? She is putting me to a test. She has been observing me for a long time. She knows everything about me. It's I who am unable to know anything about her. I'm living in ignorance. On the day I come to know everything about her and get rid of my ignorance, I'll acquire the qualification to make her my own. Only then, she will welcome me. Only then, she and I will be united,' Mohan went on speaking seriously.

I felt uneasy and concerned for him. 'Orey Mohan, you're losing your mind. When I look at you, I really....'

'You'll surely think so, I know. Wait for ten days, you'll understand why I am speaking like this. Within ten days, wherever she is on the earth, I'll reach her and make her my own.'

'What'll you do with the one you already have?'

'I think, I already told you. I'll divorce her.'

'I pity you....'

'Why?'

'Seeing you ruin your own life, chasing mirages.'

'I'm not ruining my life. I'm rebuilding my ruined life,' Mohan said and walked away.

✡ ✡ ✡

Ten days passed.

In the meantime Aruna came and, as always, stayed only for a couple of days. I had been to Hyderabad for Dassera holidays.

Immediately after my return, Mohan asked me to get into his car and started telling me excitedly, 'Orey mama, I've been eagerly waiting for you. I have to tell you something very important.'

I saw new light in his eyes. He must have met the girl he had been searching. Did she really exist? Did he really meet her? Mohan drove the car to the outskirts of the town and parked it by the side of the road. 'Orey, can you believe, at least now, that the girl I love really exists?' He said and pulled out an envelope from his pocket and gave it to me. 'I got this cover yesterday by post. Read the letter in it. I've not shown this letter to anybody else.'

I opened the letter and read it.

My Dear Mohan,

You are wondering who I am, aren't you? I pity you, my dear. You are unable to recognize me. No matter how hard I try to draw you to me, you are unable to reach me. From your ignorance and from this narrow world, you are not able to emerge. I have stepped into this world for you, only for you. You are unable to recognize one who has been searching for you for ages.

What an ignoramus you are, my dear!

You are unable to reach the hands, which have been stretched out for you. You are unable to chase away the thickly sedimented darkness in you with the light in my smiles that are meant only for you. Until you know me and reach me, I won't be available to you.

I am giving you one last chance.

You can see me on the 16th of this month at Sridevi Theatre. At exactly six in the evening, I will be at the fifteen-rupee booking counter. You should recognize me yourself and say, 'Hello, I've been searching for you.' You will be then treated to the familiar smile of mine. We will then go in your car into the world all our own.

You must come exactly at six. If you are early or late by one minute, you won't see me.

This time I won't be smiling or waving my hand as usual on seeing you. You should recognize me yourself and talk to me. If you really love me, if your love is true and noble, you can easily recognize me. You must win this little test to prove your love for me. If you don't win, I will go away like Urvashi who deserted Pururava.

Waiting every minute for you, for ages....

Yours,
Manorama

PS. This letter is a top secret. Don't show it to anybody. If you show it, you will never see me.

I finished reading the letter and looked at Mohan. He seized it from my hands and returned it to the safety of his pocket.

I wanted to examine the script of the letter. It was written in a neat hand, taking pain to write every letter beautifully.

'Would you let me read the letter again?' I asked.

'It was a mistake to give it to you the first time itself... Would I give you again?' Mohan said patting his pocket. 'Do you believe me at least now?' He looked at me triumphantly.

'I don't believe you now, but on the 16th at the theatre, if the girl gets into your car, I'll believe you,' I said.

'Ahaha, come to the theatre and keep watching us from a distance... You can see for yourself, how she will get into my car.'

'Okay, all the best.'

✡ ✡ ✡

The sixteenth was a whole week away. Mohan made a big fuss these seven days. He got a new dress made. He took great care of his appearance. He got his car neatly washed so that it shone like a mirror. Wherever he went, his eyes searched for his girl. Whenever he saw a beautiful woman, his heart missed a beat.

He strongly believed that his Manorama was following him like a shadow. He felt, wherever he went, whatever he did, she was observing him. 'How long will you delude me? I'll surely get you this time,' he mumbled and felt as though he was speaking to her. 'Once we get married, we'll go on a honeymoon. You must tell me where we should go.... Did you say, where will you bring the money from? I'll sell the car. I'll mortgage the house.'

He spent the week dreaming of her. I was afraid that he might go mad before the sixteenth.

It was the sixteenth day of the month at long last.

I reached Sridevi Talkies exactly at five-fifty-five. There wasn't much rush at the booking counters. It was an old picture. People came at long intervals and in ones and twos, bought tickets and walked straight into the cinema hall.

I looked at my watch for the fifth time in five minutes. It was already six. Two not particularly good-looking girls came in a rickshaw and proceeded to the booking counter. Neither of them could have been Mohan's dream girl. I turned to the gate and waited for Mohan's car to zoom in. It was one minute past six, and to my surprise, there was no trace of Mohan. Why was he late? What would happen to him if he didn't find his girl when he came?

It was past six... two minutes... three minutes... four minutes.... Then raced in Mohan's car through the gate. People looked in surprise at the car, which came in at such a high speed.

Mohan quickly parked the car and almost ran to the fifteen-rupee booking counter.

There was nobody there.

Mohan took a close look at every female face in the theatre compound for a few minutes. His eyes did not stay on anyone for long. In the meantime, a somewhat good-looking young woman, aged about twenty, came to the booking counter. Mohan's face lit up. He looked straight into her eyes and said, 'Hello.'

The next minute, the girl's husband who had gone to park his scooter, came there and looking suspiciously at Mohan, said, 'Who are you? What do you want?'

Mohan was confused. 'Sorry... sorry,' he murmured and quickly moved away from there. For another twenty minutes, he stood observing people coming in and going out. His Manorama did not come!

It was half past six. I walked upto Mohan and stood by his side. On looking at me, his eyes came to be filled with tears. 'There has been a big mistake,' he said incoherently.

'What is that?'

'I came four minutes late. My car got involved in a minor accident on the way here. A rickshaw came in my way all of a sudden. I rammed into it. I thought the rickshaw-puller was dead. Nothing happened to him, but the rickshaw was badly damaged. Many rickshaw-pullers gathered there and started making trouble. By the time I got rid of them by throwing a hundred rupee-note at them, it was too late. She went away. I failed her test once again....'

'Mohan, don't try to deceive yourself any more. I came here five full minutes before six and stood near the booking counter. Eversince, except the girl to whom you said 'Hello,' no great beauty has come here. After all, there should be a Manorama in this world, for her to come here. The letter you received is a big fraud...It's somebody's mischief.'

'No, no, it's not fraud...not somebody's mischief. The letter was written by her. My Rama wrote it. My Manorama wrote it. My Manorama is there, waiting to be discovered. She came for me, but because I didn't come here on time, she disappeared. She punished me. That's it... that should be it... I'm a fool... an unfortunate fellow. My Manorama won't forgive me for failing in such small test.' Mohan's face contorted with pain. He looked lost and devoid of life. He could stop himself from sobbing only with a huge effort.

'Okay Mohan, would you listen to what I've to say?' I said in an effort to divert his attention.

'No...don't tell me anything. Showing you the letter itself was bad enough. She must have come to know about it. That's also one of the reasons for her not coming,' Mohan said gruffly. He then walked to his car, got into it and drove off as rashly as when he came there.

✡ ✡ ✡

A week went by.

During this week, Mohan kept roaming the streets of the town in utter helplessness. He used his car mostly for searching for the girl, squandered a lot of money on petrol, stopped eating and sleeping in time, often drank himself unconscious and cried loudly like a child, all the time blaming himself. I felt it was not possible for anybody to reform him.

One day I was going to college. Mohan's friend Gopal, who also ran a taxi, met me on the way and said, 'Sir, I've something important to speak with you.'

'What's the matter?' I asked.

'Let's go and sit in that cafe for a while.' He led me to a cafe that was slightly removed from the road. I saw Gopal with Mohan many times. They were good friends. They always went to films and hotels together. Gopal too passed B.A. like Mohan, he too took a bank loan to buy a taxi.

We entered the cafe and sat at a vacant table. 'What's it? Tell me quickly. It's time for me to go to college,' I said.

'Mohan is ruining his life, sir,' he began. 'He is not using his car as a taxi any longer, but aimlessly roaming the streets of the town. For the past two months, he has not paid the instalments of the loan either.'

'Yes, I know. I tried to reason with him many times, but he just wouldn't listen to me. It seems a certain Manorama wrote a mischievous letter to him. With that, he's been wandering like a madcap in search of her.'

'Forgive me, but it's I who wrote the letter under Manorama's name, sir,' Gopal said. There was pain in his voice.

'You! Why did you do a thing like that?' I said in utter disbelief.

'Mohan used to tell me all the time that at the bus-stand a beautiful girl waved to him and that at Sridevi Talkies a girl, no less beautiful than actress Sridevi herself, smiled at him. I got the idea of writing that letter to play a prank on him. It's not even a letter I wrote myself. Some time ago, I was going through a weekly and I came across the letter in a story. When I read it, I felt it would be a good idea to write a letter like that to Mohan. I carefully copied the letter, making but few changes, and posted it to him. I never imagined, he would take it so seriously and ruin his life like this,' Gopal explained in detail.

'Why haven't you told him about it one of all these days?'

'When has he given me the opportunity of telling him, sir? I've already told him jokingly that I wrote the letter, but he wouldn't believe a word of it.'

'You are right. He doesn't easily believe,' I agreed with him.

We sat there silently, lost in thought, for a minute.

It was Gopal who broke the silence. 'I still have the rough draft of the letter with me, sir.'

'He may believe you at least when he sees the draft. Come with it at five in the evening. We'll take him to some hotel and explain the truth to him in a way he understands,' I said and stood up to go.

Gopal too got to his feet and said, 'Okay sir. I'll come at five. Please see to it that he stays home at that time.'

That day, when I returned from college at five, Mohan was luckily at home. 'I want to speak about something important with you. Let's go out,' I proposed.

'What's it about?' Mohan asked.

'About your Manorama.'

'How are you concerned about Manorama?'

'I've come to know who your Manorama is.'

'Really? Where is she? Has she forgiven me? Did she speak to you?' Mohan shot a barrage of questions at me. Hope, distress and emotion were mingled in his voice.

'I'll tell you everything, but first let's go out.'

'Okay. Let's go right now.'

By the time we locked the door, Gopal came and joined us. We three sat in Gopal's car and reached Ashoka Hotel. After settling down at a table, I started speaking. 'Mohan, fantasy is more appealing than reality. If we don't get rid of it as early as possible, we'll be ruining our own lives,' I said, looking at Mohan.

Mohan looked disappointed. 'Isn't this what you have been preaching all these weeks? Have you brought me here only to tell me this?' He got up to go.

'Sit down, Mohan. Do you want to go even before we tell you who your Manorama is? Who do you think has written the letter to you?' I paused and said, pointing a finger at Gopal, 'It's Gopal.' But I could see that Mohan did not comprehend my words in the least. He sat there like a statue. He looked at Gopal and me by turns, silently. 'It's true, Mohan,' I went on. 'Try to understand. Just to have some fun at your cost, Gopal himself has written the letter to you. If you want, you can compare the script of the letter with Gopal's handwriting.'

Gopal took a hint from me and said, 'I have the draft of the letter with me. Look at this.' He pulled out a piece of paper from his pocket and proffered it to Mohan. Mohan didn't take it. He abruptly rose from his seat, caught hold of Gopal's collar and started beating him with all his strength. 'Who the bloody hell are you? What's there between you and my Manorama? If you play any more tricks on me, I'll kill you, cut you into pieces. You son of a bitch,' he shouted.

I was nonplused at what had happened before I could bat an eyelid. For a few moments I didn't know what to do. I then said, recovering my poise, 'Mohan, what's this? Leave him... Leave him.' I tried my best to separate them. All the people sitting in the hotel were staring at us.

Mohan continued to shout, 'That letter was not written by him. Manorama herself wrote it. You've plotted to separate me from my Manorama. But you can't fool me. Nobody in the world can rob me of my Manorama.' Mohan still held Gopal's collar.

Gopal struggled to free himself. 'I swear on our favourite god, Yadagiri Narasimha Swamy. I wrote the letter myself'.

The next second, Mohan's hand made a violent contact with

Gopal's cheek. Like a mad man, Mohan pounced on Gopal and resumed beating him.

I once again made an effort to disengage them. 'Mohan, have you gone mad?' I said pushing him away from Gopal.

'Yes, I've gone mad. You two are making me mad by telling me lies about my Manorama.' Mohan swung his shoulders. 'Orey Gopal, if you tell me any more lies about the letter, I'll make you disgorge blood and break your bones. Beware!' Mohan screamed and stormed out of the hotel.

People gathered around us and started enquiring what was wrong.

Gopal and I looked at each other and walked out of the hotel with bent heads.

"Manorama"

Trans. M. Rajeshwar & D.V. Ramani

# BEGGAR

After attending a wedding in a relative's family at a village near Kothagudem, I started my journey back to Warangal. Assuming that travel by the Singareni Express, that plied between Kothagudem and Bellampalli, would be comfortable, I woke up at four o'clock, caught a bus by four-thirty and reached Kothagudem by six-fifteen. Only fifteen minutes time was still left for the train to start.

I hopped off the bus and almost ran to the railway station. Being in a big hurry to buy a ticket and board the train, I was startled to see a long queue at the booking counter. The train stood on the platform, ready to leave. I could see that it was impossible to get a ticket within fifteen minutes under the circumstances. Still, since I could do nothing about it, I stood in the queue. I have always felt it irritating to stand in queues for long.

The queue was moving tardily. Within two or three minutes, another ten people came and stood behind me.

I found my patience depleting by the minute. I even thought of informing the ticket collector and boarding the train. Only another five minutes time was left for the train to start.

'Where do you want to go, sir?' I heard someone say as if to greet me and turned back. A neatly dressed young man of about twenty-five was looking at me with a smile on his lips. He said, 'Haven't you recognized me, sir?'

'No,' I said, trying to recall who he was.

'I was your student, sir. I studied at Arts and Sciences College in Warangal. At present I'm working as an SI at Palvancha.'

'Oh, really? What's your name?' I said surprised. I was still trying to place him.

'I'm Bhaskar, sir. Tell me where you are going. I will arrange to get a ticket for you. There's hardly any time.'

I gave him a ten-rupee note and said, 'Warangal.'

Bhaskar called the constable standing at the booking counter and asked him to buy a ticket to Warangal. My mind was still struggling to refresh my memory of the man who suddenly materialised there to set me free from the queue. Eversince I joined as a lecturer, hundreds of students might have taken their degrees and left the college. How many of them could I remember? This tall and well-built Bhaskar was coming closest to being recognized and was then fading out in my mind. Suddenly, my eyes fell upon the copy of *The Indian Express* Bhaskar held in his hand. As soon as I saw Gavaskar's picture on the last page. I said with great relief, 'You used to play cricket at college, am I right Bhaskar?'

'Yes, sir. I was selected to play for the university too,' he replied.

'Yes, now I remember you very well. During one of the cricket matches you played, I even did running commentary for a while.'

'Yes, sir,' he said.

Meanwhile, the constable brought a ticket and gave it to Bhaskar.

I took it from him and said, 'Thank you Bhaskar, thank you very much.'

'You better hurry, sir. The train is already jam-packed. I wonder whether you'll get a seat...,' he said apprehensively.

'Aren't you coming, Bhaskar?' I asked.

He said, 'No, sir. I came here to see a friend off.'

I thanked him again and hurried along the platform. The fight for tickets at the counter turned violent. I congratulated myself for escaping the melee and started looking into compartment after compartment for a vacant seat. There appeared to be no hope of finding a seat anywhere. Resigning myself to the prospect that further search for a seat was futile, I entered a compartment and looked around for a small place to sit on. I scanned every face in the compartment in the hope of finding somebody like Bhaskar who would offer me a seat. I found nobody who would welcome me. But my attention was drawn to a seat. It was large enough to accommodate five people, but a woman occupied it with her many items of luggage. Hoping to find some room to sit, by moving the luggage, I walked upto the seat.

The woman sitting there appeared to be very poor, a beggar. She wore tattered clothes that hung loose from her body. On the seat opposite her sat two boys and two girls. From their bodies too hung tattered clothes. It didn't take long for me to understand that they were her children. They were all dirty and looked repulsive. The stench of sweat coming from their bodies was unbearable. I felt afraid of sitting by their side. But there was no other go — it was better to sit beside them than to stand for three long hours.

'Look here, if you keep these things on the floor, another two or three people can sit,' I suggested to the woman politely.

'Nothing doing. I won't remove my things. Go and sit in another compartment. Have you found only us?' she replied rudely. Her hair, which was dry like hay due to non-application of oil, her yellowed teeth, her deeply sunken and small eyes, and her belly announcing her pregnancy — on looking at her, I felt I would run into the danger of hating the entire womankind itself. I felt like leaving the place at once, but a passenger who sat nearby said loudly to the woman, 'You good for nothing bitch of a beggar! If you guttersnipes are so arrogant, how proud should we be? How politely has the *sar* asked you for a seat! If you keep the luggage on the floor, will it be soiled? Does your grand father own this train? Or your father? Remove that junk from the seat and allow the *sar* to sit.' He wore khaddar clothes and it was possible that he was a big political leader.

With the gentleman's intervention she came down a bit, and

putting one of the several bundles down on the floor, she said, 'My man has gone to get tickets. Won't he need a seat when he comes? We kept a seat for him.' She looked at me as if suggesting that I should sit there now.

I pushed my suitcase onto the rack above and squeezed myself into the little place offered to me. The woman's children, sitting opposite me, began to look at me as though I were their enemy. I felt a little guilty when it occurred to me that these children were probably thinking that I usurped the province they had gained through hard work.

I took a close look at their luggage lying heaped on the seat and beneath it. It appeared to me that they were moving house to a different place. Cooking utensils, torn mats, coarse beds, frames and legs of cots, old umbrellas, lanterns, empty bottles, kerosene containers, fire wood and many other things lay scattered around.

The guard blew his whistle. I looked at my watch. It was six-thirty-five — five minutes late. The next instant, the train hooted.

'Where is your father? Is he dead? The train is starting....' The woman's voice was full of anxiety and agitation. Her husband had not returned with the tickets yet. I looked out of the window. At the booking counter, there were still many people. Soon I saw a middle aged man running towards our compartment. On seeing him the children stood and cried out happily, 'Father is coming, father is coming.'

The man was clearly in distress. He shouted, 'Couldn't get tickets. The train is moving. Get the luggage out and get down you too.'

On hearing this, the children and the woman started wailing loudly.

Once again the khaddar-clad gentleman intervened. 'You silly son of donkey! Will the train wait until you get this cart load of luggage out? Why did you board the train without tickets? Go and request the TTI *garu* and then get in.'

'There, I've given money to my fellow for buying tickets.

Won't the money be gone if I board the train and go away?' he said and ran to the booking counter again.

The train hooted again and started pulling out of the station.

Seeing the man run to the counter, instead of boarding the train, his children and wife started fretting again.

'You too better get off the train. If the TTI comes, he'll fine you heavily,' one of the passengers advised the woman.

I said, 'How can they get down with so much luggage after the train has started moving?'

'Let that fellow go; he'll come by another train,' the leader said to the woman. 'If by chance the TTI comes, do you have the money to pay fine?'

'Ayyo Dora, I don't have even a paisa, I'm your salve,' she said weeping.

'You'll say like that, I know. These days even people like us don't have the kind of money you beggars have. What cares do you have? Yours is a business without capital,' the leader continued.

People sitting all around laughed at the remark.

I felt like shouting, 'How can you laugh at them when they are so terrified' but I checked myself because I was afraid that if I did say so they would take me for a madcap and laugh at me too.

The train had not picked up speed yet.

We saw the woman's husband coming towards us, running fast along the platform. His crying children paused and shouted, 'Ayya, ayya.' He ran faster and got into the compartment. The children felt relieved. He came to where we were sitting. He was panting. He might be around fifty. He wore a turban on his head. He had many days' of growth on his face. Half of his beard was gray. His moustaches were long and bushy. His eyes were bloodshot and looked like the embers of tamarind wood. On looking at him, one would think that he had been suffering from some disease for a long time. He wore a *banian* that had many holes in it and a *dhoti* above his knees. The stench of cigar hit us when he came near.

His wife asked eagerly, 'Have you brought tickets?'

'How could I? While I was running towards the counter, the train started moving. Seeing the train moving, I turned back. The tickets are gone and the money is gone,' he said.

'What'll you do if the TTI comes?' the leader asked him.

'I'll fall at his feet.'

'Will he pardon you, if you fall at his feet?'

'What else can I do, sir?'

'You people are better off... wherever it is, you can beg... easy life, without having to spend a pie.'

Others started taking part in the conversation.

A passenger said, 'All the towns are theirs... All the countries are theirs. They eat when they get food; otherwise they starve. They live without a care. They are better off when compared to us.'

Another said, 'I read in the papers some time ago. It seems there are bank accounts in the names of beggars. They have five thousand, ten thousand to their credit!'

'If the TTI comes, he'll surely make them pay fine or throw them out at the next station,' yet another passenger chimed in.

Unmindful of all this, the woman wailed, 'Wretched fellow! Had gone for a whole hour and returned without tickets. Says he'd given the money to somebody there!'

'People were jostling and fighting at the counter. What could I do, you woman? The one who came with us, my brother's son, I gave him the money and asked him to buy tickets. While I stood watching the train...' he trailed off.

'Ayyo! Let your hands break! Have you given the money to that thief? How could you believe him? Ayyo, ayyo...thirty rupees,' she started beating her chest.

'Was he also to travel with you?' the leader asked the man.

'No, I'm your slave. He lives in Palvancha. He came here to see us off. I'm not well and I've come here for a check-up at hospital. Your slave. For the last two months, cough, incessant cough,' the beggar said and started coughing his lungs out.

His wife said, 'He'll take the thirty rupees and go straight to a liquour shop. He won't return a single pie to you.'

'He is not that sort. He'll buy tickets.'

The leader said again, 'What's the use of buying tickets after the train has left. It'll be all right if he informs the station master that he bought tickets. But does he know such things?'

The train stopped at a station. As has been feared, the TTI walked into our compartment. On seeing him, the woman started weeping. The children joined her.

A passenger said, 'Here, in this jungle, he'll throw you out.'

Another passenger said, 'No, he won't do that. He'll ask them to get out at the next station.'

The TTI came to our seats, checking the passengers' tickets row after row. We showed him our tickets. But the beggar raised his folded hands.

'It's not to me you should raise your folded hands. Do that to God above. Stop these tricks and show me the tickets,' the TTI thundered.

'Ayya, I wanted to buy tickets. Today at the Kothagudem station, there was a large crowd. I sent my brother's son to buy tickets. As he put his hand into the counter, the train started moving. I left him there and rushed to board the train..., 'the beggar explained.

But the railway officer paid no attention to his words. He said, 'Shut up, you thief! I know only too well about people like you. Where are you going?'

The TTI was a middle-aged man. He seemed to be well experienced in matters like this. Speaking rudely and harshly appeared to be a very natural thing for him.

The beggar said, 'Nekkonda, your slave.'

These children and the woman, are they yours?' asked the TTI.

'Ayya, they are mine.'

'Then, come out with fifty six rupees.'

The beggar immediately stooped and clasped the feet of the TTI.

'Get up, you son of a donkey. Why do you touch my feet? Are you giving me the money or shall I hand you over to the police?' the TTI said freeing his feet.

'Even if you cut me into pieces, you can't find a pie on me, your slave. I gave all my money to him.'

'Who is he?'

'He is my brother's son. I gave him thirty rupees for the tickets.' The beggar attempted to fall at his feet again.

He swiftly moved away. 'Your tricks won't work on me. Are you taking out fifty-six rupees or not?' he said looking down on him severely.

I was watching all this keenly. I felt I should somehow help the beggar out. I said in English to the TTI, 'TT *garu*, why don't you listen to what he has been saying? Today, there was really a heavy rush at the booking counter at the Kothagudem station. It seems he gave money to someone there. Even before he brought the tickets, the train started moving. Out of the anxiety that his wife, children and luggage were left in the train, he boarded it without another thought.'

My speaking in English had the effect of softening the sternness of the TTI. He said, 'Then we'll do like this: at the next station, I'll make a phone call to the station master at Kothagudem. I'll ask him if anybody has returned tickets meant for Nekkonda. If what this man is saying is true, those tickets must have been returned. If the station master says the tickets have been indeed returned, he'll have no problem. Orey, what's your name?' He looked at the beggar.

'Brahmaiah, your slave.'

'What's the name of that other fellow you gave the money to at Kothagudem?'

'Somaiah, your slave.'

'Within five minutes, I'll prove to you whether he is telling the truth or playing a trick,' the TTI said looking at me.

Everybody in the compartment started discussing this issue animatedly.

A man said, 'I wonder if he knew he should return the tickets. It's possible that he went away after the train had left the station.'

'Abbo, these days, nobody is so very innocent,' another passenger added.

Meanwhile the train reached another station.

'Orey Brahmaiah, come with me,' the TTI said and took the beggar away with him.

My fellow passengers eagerly waited for the outcome. They continued to speak among themselves.

'Ah! He could not have been so very intelligent. After the train had left, he must have gone away keeping the tickets in his pocket.'

'He might not have bought the tickets at all. Seeing the train depart, he must have pocketed the money and left.'

'He is that sort of man, your slave. He must have gone to a liquor shop,' Brahmaiah's wife agreed with him.

Five minutes before the train was to resume its journey, the TTI boarded the train along with Brahmaiah. He declared loudly, 'Haven't I said, it's all play-acting! The station master at Kothagudem has just told me that nobody had come to return tickets. Orey Brahmaiah, at least now give me the money.'

Brahmaiah started wailing. His wife and children joined him.

'If you cry and make a noise, I'll get you skinned. Dirty scoundrels... rogues... shut up,' the TTI barked.

Brahmaiah and his family were terrified. They fell silent immediately.

'Orey Brahmaiah, come out with the money,' the TTI said again.

'Ayya, even if you cut me into pieces you can't find any money on me,' Brahmaiah said and swung at his feet.

'If you touch me, I'll kill you... badmash! Luchcha! Isn't there any money on you? Take out the turban,' shouted the TTI.

Forthwith the man accompanying him, who looked like his attendant, put out his hand to pull Brahmaiah's turban. Brahmaiah took two steps away and held his turban tightly with both his hands. He said, 'What's there in this turban, your slave? I got it in alms from a Dora like you. Believe me, your slave. Allow me to get off the train at the next station, your slave.' He burst out coughing. Paying no heed to his words the railway officer moved forward and pulled his turban. Brahmaiah tried to protect his turban from coming off by calling up all his energy. But his effort went waste. In the tussle between him and the officer, the turban was torn and three currency notes fell down from it. On seeing them, the TTI's eyes shone brightly. The passengers looked at the money with wide eyes — if any sympathy had built up in their hearts for Brahmaiah so far, it got evaporated that minute.

The khaddar-clad leader said, 'Thieving son of a bitch! Must not believe them at all! The TTI *garu* knew about them only too well. He has done the right thing.' Others in the compartment also felt like him. The assistant picked up the three ten-rupee notes and placed them in the TTI's hands. He immediately transferred them to his pocket. 'Aren't these the thirty rupees you gave your brother's son?' he said infusing into his words as much sarcasm as possible.

The travellers burst out laughing.

'No lord, no. The money I gave him has been lost there itself,' Brahmaiah grovelled.

'Chutt! Bloody scoundrel... still trying to cheat me... take out... the rest of 26 rupees too...'

'Beat us to pulp...kill us...throw us out of the moving train... still, you can't find any money on us,' Brahmaiah's wife said going to the aid of her husband.

'Shut up, you bitch. If you have no money, who'll pay the fine? Pull out that pouch hanging to your waist,' the TTI said looking daggers at her.

'What's there in it, your slave? Just change, collected

begging for the last couple of days,' she said placing a hand on the pouch.

'Let me see, what's there in it? Give it to me,' the TTI insisted.

'Ayya, allow us to keep at least enough to buy beaten rice. We haven't eaten anything for the past two days. My man is being laid waste by some disease. Look at my children! They are dying of hunger. I touch your feet, your slave.' She stood up and got ready to walk up to the TTI.

It surprised me that the people in the compartment felt animosity towards the pregnant woman, instead of pity, an animosity that was born of the belief that the poor wretch deserved to be treated the way she was being treated. If such a scene were to be shown in a film, they would all be moved to tears. What is the reason for such self-contradiction in people? It may be that they felt jealous because they had to buy tickets for the journey while the beggars were trying to get away without buying any. Perhaps such conflict between the travellers who bought tickets and those who haven't, is inevitable! They can't forget on these occasions that 'they are travellers.' While watching a film, they don't think like travellers. At such times the sympathy, compassion, and pity, which are natural to human beings, are activated in them.

While I was still lost in thoughts like this, the TTI snatched the dirty pouch hanging to the beggar woman's waist. He poured its contents onto the floor. Some one-rupee notes; some five-rupee notes? the rest change — five-paise coins, ten-paise coins... The TTI quickly counted the money and took away twenty-six rupees from it. Apart from two ten-paise coins and three five-paise coins, nothing was left there. The TTI's assistant picked them up and offered them to the beggar woman.

'Let him keep them too,' she said indignantly.

The TTI was infuriated at these words. 'I'll hit you with a *chappal*, you thieving bitch! Why would I take your beggarly coins? The bitch has put on fat, eating free food. You won't learn a lesson unless I hand you over to the police, put you in lock-up for a few days and get you properly beaten,' he hissed and ground his teeth.

Brahmaiah rushed to take the money. He said, his hands folded, 'Foolish woman! She doesn't know any thing. Please forgive us, babu.'

The TTI, who had been standing all this while, requested me to move a bit and sat beside me. He took out from his pocket what looked like a receipt-book. He quickly scribbled something in it in pencil.

The train was approaching Dornakal.

The TTI tore a slip off the book and said, giving it to Brahmaiah, 'Look here! Keep this receipt with you and show it when you alight from the train at Nekkonda.' While he was pressing the piece of paper into Brahmaiah's hands, my eyes fell upon it. '22 rupees...Dornakal to Nekkonda' was what I could see.

I thought I understood something.

The train stopped at the Dornakal station.

The TTI quickly got down from the compartment and walked away.

I wanted to tell my fellow passengers what I understood. But again I felt, in a country where such things had become the order of the day, no useful purpose would be served by sharing my knowledge of the TTI's dishonesty with them.

For a long time, I kept thinking about Brahmaiah and the railway officer.

Of the two, who was the worse beggar?

"Bichchagadu"
Trans. C.L.L. Jayaprada

# PARADISE LOST

AP Express, which was scheduled to reach Secunderabad by 8 o'clock in the evening, was approaching the station one hour late. Sukumar held his suitcase and holdall in his hands and was ready to alight from the train as soon as it came to a halt. As the train approached Secunderabad, impatience built up within him. After Ramagundam, the train had to stop for a long time waiting for the signal to be given or some such technical problem. It was a vexatious and painful wait for Sukumar. Ananya came to his mind every second. She must be sitting all alone, waiting for him to return. By now, she must have rung up the station any number of times. They must have told her that the train was late by an hour. She must have been waiting for him impatiently like one sitting on fire. She must have even come to the station by now.

Sukumar had to go to Delhi even before their marriage entered the second month. The company for which he worked as a manager had its head office in Delhi. The MD called him to Delhi to discuss the measures to improve sales. He made it clear to Sukumar that he should come prepared to stay for more than four days in Delhi. Sukumar knew, whatever reason he gave, the trip to Delhi could not be postponed. So, it was with great reluctance that he went to Delhi. The separation from Ananya for so many days was very painful.

At the head office in Delhi, there was a meeting everyday. The progress made by the company for the past one decade, charts indicating sales, measures to improve them further, incentives, ads — with discussions on all these his mind was distracted.

When he returned to the hotel everyday in the evening, he

used to remember Ananya. He eagerly waited for the meetings to come to an end so that he could go to Hyderabad, to his Ananya. He spent time counting every minute and every hour. The memories of Ananya permitted him no sleep.

After their marriage, he spent hardly ten days with Ananya. She was in Karimnagar with her parents and he in Hyderabad. He had been to see her only at the week-ends. Of late however, his father-in-law had bought a big house for them at Banjara Hills in Hyderabad. They moved into the house but had hardly had the time to settle down before he left for Delhi.

He had not understood Ananya so far. There was no time for it. They wanted to go on a honeymoon following the marriage, but the idea had to be shelved because he didn't get leave from work. The marriage itself took place in a hurry and there was no time to plan things in advance.

Ananya... his darling Ananya! Could she have been waiting for him at the station? Suddenly he remembered his friend Ravikanth's words at the Delhi railway station. Ravikanth was his childhood friend. He had a job in Delhi. He came to the station to see him off. While in Delhi he had been to Ravi's house and had dinner with him and his wife. Ravi too was married not long back. Sukumar was delighted to see this couple. They seemed to get along famously with each other, making jokes about each other all the time and filling their house with hearty laughter and banter.

Ravikanth had said, 'Of all the people I know, you are the first man to come to Delhi days after marriage and leaving the wife behind. Look at me, I never left the side of my wife for at least six months after we were married.'

'What could I do? If I hadn't come when the MD summoned me, I could have as well lost my job,' he said in explanation.

'You should have let it go. If you lose this job, you'll get another. Don't forget, you're a B.E. and M.B.A. on top of it. Any employer would be glad to offer you a cushy job.'

I'm not so sure. What's the guarantee that I'll get another

good job so soon? Don't they say, a bird in hand is worth two in the bush?

'If you are so calculated about things you can't enjoy life. At least you could have brought your wife with you to Delhi.'

'I didn't get the idea at all. She too didn't say she'd like to come. If she insisted, I'd have perhaps brought her along.'

'That's the mistake we men folk keep making all the time. Women never ask for anything, don't express their desire to be taken anywhere. We ourselves should find out what's there on their mind and attend to their wishes.'

'Shouldn't they find out what is on our mind and fulfil our desires too?'

'Brother, that would be the sweetest thing about married life! One should know the other, fulfil each other's desires and derive joy and pleasure in life. You left that joy behind and have come away to this god-damned at Delhi. You had always been dull-witted as a boy. Do you remember, our teachers used to call you a slow-wit? Have you ever been angry with or emotional about anything?'

He laughed. 'Yes, I do get angry and emotional, but not with others. I'm often angry with myself.'

'No, no. A man should cherish anger, be emotional. He should be willing to laugh and enjoy all shades of life. I wish that at least your wife would change you. Enjoy life with her. Nothing can give a man as much pleasure as a woman can give,' Ravi said.

After he had boarded the train, Ravikanth bid him goodbye and went away. It's true, only a woman can give a man the highest form of pleasure. But don't women get any pleasure from men? At 'that' particular moment, why does only man take the initiative? Why is that woman never tells her husband that she wants to be close to him? Had Ananya ever hugged him and said, 'Come on dear, let's make love?' He himself had to propose all the time. She would invariably say, 'Not now, wait for sometime.' He had to ask her again, persuade her, beg her and sometimes even force her. At last, she would agree to it feeling as though she was making a sacrifice for him. While it lasted, she would close her eyes and lie on the bed like a sacrificial animal, never participating, never showing any interest. Was it that Ananya alone did like that or was it common to all women?

He liked Ananya at the very first sight. On meeting her at the bridal interview, he felt she was the right life-partner for him. She was ravishingly beautiful, well educated and spoke in a lively manner. He felt she had the intelligence and refinement of spirit to understand him. Her family background too was excellent. Her father had retired as a superintending engineer. Her two brothers, one a doctor and another a business executive, had settled in the US. She was the only daughter of the family. He thought, by marrying her, he himself would get a chance to go to the USA.

Everyone in her family adored Ananya. She was brought up with tenderness and uncritical love. Sukumar's parents felt that this match was the right in every respect. He immediately agreed to the marriage and didn't specify what to be offered as dowry.

✡ ✡ ✡

The train pulled to a halt at the Secunderabad station. He came out of his compartment and saw the chauffeur Pasha running towards him. He gave him his suitcase and holdall and asked, 'Have you come alone?'

'Yes, sir,' Pasha replied.

'Hasn't anybody else come?' he said beginning to feel uncomfortable.

'No, sir.'

He thought Ananya would come to receive him at the station. He spoke to her from Delhi and specifically asked her to be at the station when the AP Express arrived in Secunderabad. She had said, in reply, 'Yes darling. I've been eagerly waiting for you. Can't you come by flight?' But she had not come! Disappointment, terrible disappointment!

He emerged from the station, and when Pasha brought the car before him, he got into it. As the car raced to his house in Banjara Hills, his mind got busy thinking. After reaching home he should imprison Ananya in his arms, should press her to his bosom with all his strength and should not let her go until she pleaded for mercy. He should tell her that it was the punishment he had awarded her for not coming to the station to receive him. He himself wouldn't be able to find freedom from the thirst, hunger, loneliness and torment of the past one week unless he united with her.

Half an hour later the car drew to a halt in the portico of the house. He expected Ananya to wait for him at the gate itself. But she wasn't there. He got off the car and waited in the portico; Ananya might come running any moment! But she didn't come. After an uneasy wait for a couple of minutes he entered the house — Ananya didn't appear to be at home at all! He lowered himself into a sofa and slowly took off his shoes. The cook Sujata came and stood in front of him. She said, 'Madam has gone out, sir. She would be back in about half an hour.'

Gone out? She had gone out even when she knew that he was returning home after a whole week! What was the urgent work? Was it more important than to receive him and to relieve him of his tiredness? Damn it!

He looked at the cook and said, 'I want to have a bath. Have you turned the geyser on?'

'I'll do it at once,' Sujata said and swiftly walked away.

Sukumar changed into a *lungi*. Thoughts crowded his mind again. This was preposterous! Couldn't she have postponed her work for the sake of her husband who had been longing to see her every minute of a week, who had travelled 1500 kilo metres and for twenty eight hours in the hope of resting in her lap? Was this the same woman whom he thought of as his partner in life, his better half, at the very first sight; the embodiment of love with whom he wanted to share his woes and joys, his dreams and tears all through his life? But who wanted him to think the way he did about her? He had imagined everything himself. How difficult it is to judge a person based on mere appearance! What is the guarantee that people with beautiful bodies also have beautiful hearts?

Sukumar entered the bathroom and turned on the shower. It felt good to have warm water running down his body. In Delhi, the winter was terrifying. How many times he had felt, if only Ananya were with him... if only he slept hugging her — how warm it would have been! Would that wish be fulfilled at least today? Would Ananya return home at all? Would he see her? Would his dream come true? He shampooed his hair. He expected Ananya would rub shampoo into his hair and pour warm water over him. He wished that she would apply soap to his back and tickle his ribs.

Why did Ananya do this? What happened to her? Where could she have gone? To a film? To a friend's house? Or her father's place? Would she return? Would she rescue him from the pyre of loneliness?

He wiped himself on a towel and wrapped it around him. He then walked to the dressing table and standing before it, dusted powder all over his face and shoulders. Later he went and sat in a chair in front of the TV. He flipped through many channels but didn't feel like watching any. He turned the TV off. How nice would it be if Ananya came at least now!

It was past ten already.

'Shall I serve you your dinner, sir?' Sujata asked from behind him.

'Won't your mistress come for the night?'

'She told me to serve you your food in case she got delayed, sir.'

'Oh, she has asked you to serve me my food, hasn't she? Then go ahead and serve.' He rose from his chair and walked to the dining table in the centre of the hall. He placed some rice and curry in his plate and started mixing them. He felt a strange uneasiness in his chest. What was it? What was happening to him? Why was his throat getting blocked? Why was the food not going down his throat? Why was his heart becoming heavy?

*This is absurd! You are behaving like a child. Don't become a child....*

No, no... somebody had badly deceived him — otherwise, why should he get a wife like this?

*Nobody has deceived you. You are deceiving yourself. Why did you get ready to marry her with your eyes on only her good looks and wealth? Did you speak with her even for an hour before marriage? Did you find out what kind of woman she is, what likes and dislikes she has, what her outlook on life is and which values she cherishes? Did you stop to think whether compatibility was possible between you two? You had seen only her father's money, her splendid figure and the fact of her two brothers living in the US. You thought you might get a chance of going to the US yourself, didn't you?*

He felt hungry, but the food didn't taste good. He washed his hands in the plate and rose from the table.

Bedroom...AC bedroom...his heaven, but now it looked like hell. If Ananya came at least now! By now, they should be in paradise. That paradise was slipping from his hands — *paradise lost* — gone... paradise was gone.

No...no, paradise was not lost. Ananya would come. She would take care of him... relieve him of his distress in a second. He would place his head on her bosom and sleep blissfully.

Somebody was knocking at the door.

It was not locked.

Coming...Ananya was coming. He must not speak to her for a while...should pretend to be asleep.

Ananya pushed the door open and came in. The devil that had put him to torment had come. The goddess who would offer him a taste of heaven had come.

'Hello darling! When have you come?' she said coming near him. The intoxicating scent coming from her hair and body made him breathless. He felt an urge to gather her in his arms and kiss her all over the body. He might not be able to control himself much longer. Any minute his reserve might fail. He would surrender himself completely to her. No, no...he must not yield to her, for she had teased him so cruelly.

'Are you angry with me, dear?' she crooned, bringing her mouth close to his ear.

'No, I felt very happy,' he said sarcastically and turned his face away from her.

'Sorry, dear. I wanted to return home before you came. But that wretched train seems to have arrived on time.'

'It came a whole hour late.'

'Why one hour? Couldn't it have come three hours late? After all, it has been trudging all the way from Delhi.'

He said nothing.

'Are you still angry with me, dear? For your sake, to appear wonderful and divine to you, I've been to the beauty parlour. I wanted to be back in an hour, but they at the beauty parlour stretched it to three hours...'

'So it is to a beauty parlour that you have been!' He looked at her keenly and with wide observant eyes. He kept staring at her for a good few seconds in disbelief.

She blushed and said, 'What are you looking at? My friends who came from Chennai yesterday had told me that my hair-style was out of fashion. I wanted to change my hair-style before you came today and surprise you with it. So the visit to the beauty parlour.'

'Who said your hair-style was not pretty?'

'I told you they are my friends. I ran into them at Hotel Krishna Oberoi. Vandana and Chandana, my childhood friends. Their husbands came here to attend some conference and they came along. They were shocked at my hair-style. They said it suited only a middle-aged woman. They even teased me that if I continued with it, you would look for another woman. They themselves took me to the beauty parlour and brought about this transformation.' She paused and drew an imaginary circle around her head with a finger. 'Don't I look gorgeous now, dear, like a teenager?'

'Not like a teenager; you look like a granny.'

'What's this, dear? How can you speak so harshly? If you

say such things, I'll cry,' she said. Almost immediately, her eyes were filled with tears.

'When I look at you, at your hair-do, I feel like crying myself,' he said making no effort to mollify her.

'Why, dear?'

'How luxurious was your hair! Don't you remember I used to admire your long hair that fell on to your shoulders and back, spreading an intoxicating scent? I was proud of it. A woman's beauty lies in her hair? And you got it all bobbed, forgetting that you might look more like a man!'

'Who said a woman's hair is the hall mark of her beauty?' Ananya said impatiently. 'You men folk said it. Actually, who do you men think you are to talk about women's beauty? How we should look is something we should decide ourselves. This is our hair and it's our wish....'

'Then why is it that you women go to beauty parlours? Who are your beauty and charms for? Aren't they for us men? Isn't it to attract us with your beauty, to arouse us sexually and to keep us in your grip that you do all this?'

'No, not at all for you. Our beauty is for our own sake, for our happiness and for our satisfaction.'

'That's a lie, a blatant lie,' he almost shouted.

She had clips all over her hair and a layer of cream on her face. Her cheeks shone like ripe apples. He felt desire stirring up within him as he continued to look at her. But for some time, both remained silent.

'Have you had your dinner?' Ananya asked, breaking the silence.

'Haven't you left a message with the cook asking me to?'

'I thought you would be hungry after a whole day and night's journey.'

'Thanks for the concern. Have you thought of another hunger I could possibly have?'

'What's that other hunger?'

'I'll tell you later. First go and change your dress and wash those creams off your face. I can't wait.'

'Oh, you mean *that* by another hunger!'

'Yes, that's it. Go, take a bath, eat and come here without wasting much time.'

'Sorry, dear.'

'Why? Why should you be sorry?'

'I can't satisfy your 'hunger' tonight.'

'Don't talk nonsense. It's not me alone, you should also be 'hungry.' Both of us have been 'fasting' for a week. You speak as though it's something which concerns me alone.'

'I don't have 'that' hunger. Please leave me alone tonight. The beautician has asked me to keep these clips on all through the night. If they are disturbed, I won't have curls the way I want. I'll sleep in another room tonight.'

'Let your curls go to hell. I want you tonight. I want you at any cost. Please understand my agony.'

'First you try to understand my problem. Tonight it's not possible. I'm not interested.'

'You can go to another beautician tomorrow, if these curls are so important to you. Don't say no to me tonight,' he almost pleaded.

'I said I'm not interested.'

'When were you really interested in it, to be interested tonight? Look at it this way: make a sacrifice for me.'

'I made many such sacrifices in the past, but tonight I can't. Please leave me alone,' she said and rose to go.

'Ananya, don't test my patience.'

'You too don't test my patience. Please, if it is so unberable for you, take a pill and sleep.' She walked out of the room.

'Damn it!' he shouted loudly. He took the alarm time-piece from the tea-table and hurled it down. It hit the ground and broke into pieces. He picked up the pillows from the bed and threw them at the wall. He swept the cans and bottles of powders, scents and creams down from the dressing table with a hand. They fell helter-skelter.

Ananya heard the noise and came back. 'What's this naughtiness? Like a child...just one day...can't you wait for me? Can't you make this little sacrifice?' she said annoyed.

'Not for a day. I can't wait even for a second. Please... for my sake...for your husband's sake...you must sacrifice these curls. Please...' He tried to move close to her.

She swiftly moved away from him and said, 'Please wait. Control yourself. You have no right to touch me against my wish even if you are my husband.'

'Don't talk shit. About your rights and laws, I don't know. Tonight, I need you. That's all. That's what I know.' He again went near her and stretched his arms to gather her to him.

She ducked and said, 'If you compel me with your desire, there'll be serious consequences. Woman is not a machine to fulfil the sexual desire of man. She's not an object of sex any longer. You should know that.'

'You are transforming yourselves into objects of sex. Why is that you go to the beauty parlours, if not to become objects of sex?'

'How are the two related?'

'Isn't it to arouse desire in men and then make dogs out of them, wagging their tongues after you, that you attend to your beauty with such care?' It's not man who regards woman as an object of sex. Woman thinks of herself as an object of sex and ends up making herself one by visiting beauty parlours. The moment she fails to sexually attract men, she thinks of herself as a dead body. Yes, it's a fact. To encash this craze among women, beauty parlours have mushroomed in this country.

'I don't know all that. Speaking for myself, appearing beautiful is for my own sake. Don't you too want to look attractive. Don't you want women to die for you?'

'No. Like you, I've never run to a beauty parlour.' He looked straight into her eyes, somewhat mollified. 'All right, all right.

Let's make peace. Remove all that make-up at least now and come here. Let's forget everything. Let's regain paradise. Please, come on. Let's make love and be happy.'

'Impossible! I can't let you touch me tonight. Paradise won't go anywhere. You'll regain it within twenty-four hours.'

'Twenty-four hours! The world will come to an end by then. You won't be there, I won't be there. There is no tomorrow... it won't come. Now, this minute, it's real. The moment lost now won't come back. Please understand me...'

'No, please!'

'If you torture me like this, I'll go mad and the consequences will be unseemly.' There was a note of threat into his voice,

'What do you mean? What'll you do?'

'I don't know what I'll do. I may even rape you?'

'Chi, chi! Your calm and quiet exterior is misleading. I've been under the impression that you're a thorough gentleman. I never thought you'd stoop to such lowly behaviour.'

'I'm not a gentleman any longer. At the moment, I'm a devil, a brute, a beast. You should not share your life with a brute like me. Please get out. Let me not see you here another minute. Get out — go away from this house,' he screamed and hit his clenched fist against the wall.

Ananya was not much disturbed. She swung her head to a side and said, keeping her voice deliberately down, 'What right do you think you have to ask me to go away from this house? This house and everything in it have been bought by my father for me.'

'All right... all right! Everything has been bought by your father. Yes, by marrying you, I sold myself to you and your father. I deserve this punishment. It was the biggest mistake of my life to fall for your good looks and your father's money. I would like to correct myself at least now. I'm going away, leaving you and your house. I want to break the chains of slavery I put on myself at the time of marriage. I'm going away. For opening my eyes, thank you my friend... thank you. You are not my wife and I'm not your husband any more. Goodbye my friend... goodbye.' He quickly threw his clothes into his suitcase and got ready to go. 'If I take anything which is not mine, I'll have it sent to you tomorrow.' He held his suitcase in his hand and walked out of the room.

Ananya was taken by surprise at this sudden development. Showing some presence of mind, she ran after him. 'Sorry, it's not my intention to ask you to go away at this odd hour of the night. Please don't go,' she said and attempted to grab his hand.

He drew his hands away and said, 'I've understood your intention clearly enough. But I'm not angry with you now. People should know their place in life. I've fallen down trying to reach heights too lofty for me. I hold myself responsible for it. So I bear no resentment towards you,' he said with his face turned away from her.

'Please, you must not go... I swear... I'll fulfil your wish tonight. I agree to it with all my heart. Stop, please.'

Her words were lost on him. He rushed to the main door, pushed it open and emerged from the house. He banged the door shut and disappeared into the darkness of the night.

"Chejarina Swargam"

Trans. M. Rajeshwar & B. Sharmila

# SPARKS OF FIRE

Somewhere, just after midnight the dogs howled continuously, while Reddy snored, sleeping in the verandah. I lay tossing on my straw-bed outside the bungalow. Saroja would come and take me to *that* room. There, the hungry Saroja would crush me. She would ruin me completely.

Why hadn't she come tonight? The night began to grow older. The stars twinkled in the sky. The whole village fell silent. Suddenly, a bird flew over me, making an unusual sound. I trembled with fear. Somebody told me in my childhood about this bird. It is considered a spirit — a ghost. If the bird flies over a village crying like this, it will bring bad luck to it. When it cries, blood comes out of its beak and each drop of the blood causes the death of a person. My fear intensified. Reddy's snoring terrified me further. The dogs howled more frighteningly.

Saroja hadn't come yet. It was too late now. The bird flew about me again making a similar sound. My heart beat faster. My hands and legs began to tremble with fear. I felt as if the blood from its beak had fallen on me. I also felt something hitting me hard. I tried to wipe if off, but I couldn't move. I stood still. At a distance, people woke up and were trying to chase the bird away.

There was silence all around — the dogs ceased barking. Reddy might have turned to a side in his sleep; he snored less now. But Saroja hadn't come. The door of her room didn't creak. She would take me to the room — that dilapidated room where she would... Suddenly, I was overcome by fear. Saroja was a hungry tigress. She would eat me up. She would ruin my life. Reddy was a *Yama*. He would bury me alive here in the house — Saroja was a monster, Reddy an ogre. They imprisoned me here. They took delight in torturing me. I must run away from this house immediately... at this moment! But my hands and legs failed me. Saroja would come presently. She wouldn't be able to bear my separation. I pitied her... but, I should run away at once. If I stayed here any longer, I would die. In fact, death was inevitable one way or the other. The bird vomited blood on me. I wouldn't live, would I? By morning, Reddy and Saroja would cut me into pieces and bury me in the house. I hated the house with all my heart.

My coming over here took place without my knowledge or willingness. I don't know whom I was born to and where. My mother died when I was hardly three years old. And I know nothing of my father. People used to say I had no father at all. My mother worked at zamindar Ramireddy's house. After her death, I was left in his care. He fed me till I was five and I started working for him from then on. Thus, I settled down there as a servant.

I did all sorts of things for both the zamindar and his lady. Looking after their children, taking them to school and giving them a bath besides helping the lady with her daily chores like washing, cleaning and cooking, had been part of my job. I used to even massage the zamindar's legs when he retired to bed every night. They gave me only food and clothes. What more could I expect, anyway?

I don't remember exactly since when they started treating me as a fool. Everybody thought I was innocent. 'Poor fellow,' 'idiot' and 'numbskull' were some of the nicknames given to me by and by. In fact, I too pretended to be dumb. This behaviour of mine proved a blessing in disguise. I learnt to filch money whenever the lady sent me to bazaar to buy groceries. She didn't suspect me. I gradually realized the importance of money thus collected. I would walk as far as fifteen miles to buy sweets and see films. My mistress also gave me some coppers when I told her that I wanted to see a film. Several years thus went by at Ramireddy's house.

Suddenly, like a storm, Rangareddy and Saroja came into my life. Rangareddy was a big land lord of the neighbouring village. He was richer and more powerful than my master. They were distant relatives. On Ramireddy's invitation Rangareddy once visited him. I found that my master not just respected him but somehow even feared him. Soon, Rangareddy set his eyes on me.

'Is this your servant?' he enquired.

'Yes. He is just a fool. He'll do any kind of work. He needs just a little food. He's very loyal,' my master explained.

'I need a servant like that. I haven't found anyone who could work that sincerely. These servants have become headstrong now a days. On seeing me, people used to piss in their dhotis ten years ago. They used to carry out my commands without a question. Now, everyone has learnt to question. Nobody wants to work for me for more than a couple of years. Send this fellow to my village for some time. Let me see how long he'll work for me,' Rangareddy suggested.

It was thus that I came with Rangareddy to this village. But I was afraid of him. There was poison in his looks, laughter and speech. He looked terrible with his scarlet face and thick whiskers. He was six-foot tall and had a well built physique. He had small piercing eyes and a commanding voice. Children would be frightened at his sight.

Reddy's bungalow occupied a major part of the village. It was an old fashioned bungalow. The rooms and verandahs resembled the alleys in a dark cave. A part of the bungalow had been demolished. Reddy didn't get it rebuilt. He lived all alone in the large bungalow. His wife died long ago and his only daughter was away studying at college in the town.

Reddy used to assign many sundry jobs to me. I was busy doing something or the other from morning till late in the night. Of the things I did, some were inhuman, some were meant for only women and others respectable. Whatever the nature of the work, I learnt to do without complaining. Reddy felt peeved whenever he saw me doing nothing. 'You eat like a glutton, but do nothing. Idiot! Blockhead!' hurling a volley of abuse at me, he would at once find me some work to do. I would work silently, but he was never satisfied with my work. When I couldn't finish the work in time, he would shout at the top of his voice. Once or twice, he even thrashed me without a reason. He really believed that, like a pampered child, I took advantage of his 'goodness.'

I hardly moved out of the bungalow. When I went out, the villagers treated me with a lot of sympathy. They believed that I was made a sacrificial animal by Reddy. There was an ancient temple of Shiva at the centre of the village. The old man Ramayya, lived there. He was kind to me. He treated me like his son. Ramayya, like me, had no one in the world to care for him. He went into the village to beg for food and took rest at the temple. He asked me one day, 'Where are you from, my son? Are you an orphan? Haven't you found anyone other than this master? Nobody has worked for him for more than ten days so far. He wouldn't be satisfied, unless he tortures his servants.' I made no answer, but it was a great relief to go down to see him whenever time permitted.

Rangareddy had many vices. He drank and ate all the time. He would finish pots of palm-wine and bottles of liquor in no time. He flirted with women in the village. He took me with him on his 'women-hunting' trips. He would force himself into any hut that caught his fancy and I would wait outside. At times, he brought women to his bungalow. As soon as he found a helpless woman, he would force her to satisfy his lust. He had some musclemen at his disposal for this purpose.

When he drank heavily, he uttered nothing but obscenities. He would laugh to himself and say that he had a liking for teenage girls and egg-laying hens. He looked for women who were below twenty. It was believed that he had never looked at a woman past that age. He would get mischievous with the women right in front of me. He would pull their sarees, pinch their cheeks and hug them. If any woman warned him, 'Look, that fellow is watching' he would say, 'So what? He is just a child. Do you know... at times when there is no woman around, I sleep with him.' He would then let out a loud guffaw.

This made my blood boil. I didn't know what my age was then. Probably, I was eighteen or nineteen, but I looked much younger in my banian and knickers.

He used to ask every woman who came to his bungalow for her age. On being told that she was still sixteen or seventeen, he would feel very happy and say proudly, 'you are exactly my Saroja's age.' As he said this he would wear the look of satisfaction of realizing a dream. Everyone knew about Reddy's weakness for women, but they talked about it only among themselves.

Saroja came from the town a month after my moving to this village. She closely resembled her father. When I saw her, I experienced a sense of fear. It was like meeting Reddy all over again. Like her father, Saroja too was brawny and proportionately built. Looking at men out of the corner of her eye, she would make one feel as though she would eat one up alive. There was an air of pride and carelessness about her bearing.

When she saw me, she cried out in surprise, 'Oh! You are the new servant! Good.' She then turned to her father and said, 'I like him. Where did you find this strange beast, father?'

'I brought him from Ranagareddy's house. He is a proper simpleton. He'll be of general help to you,' Reddy replied.

As soon as she settled down, Saroja made my life miserable by asking me to do all kinds of work. What surprised me more was Reddy's unnatural love for her. Though considered hard-hearted, Reddy melted to tears when she came back from the town. He embraced her and said, 'You've become very thin, my darling. Wasn't the food at the hostel good? Did they serve chicken at least once a week? Did you work hard, paying no attention to your health?' Making many such enquiries, he was all care for her all that day and I could see that he fulfilled her every fancy in the days that followed.

When the visiting villagers asked him when he was going to get his daughter married, Reddy would fly into a rage.

'Marriage... marriage!... you don't seem to be satisfied unless she marries even before she reaches sixteen, bears children and becomes a hag while she is still in her twenties. I won't get her married now. She must pass her B.A. and M.A. What do you think of my daughter? She's a princess! She'll keep up my image. Do you think, like an ordinary woman, she would get married and have children? It's just impossible,' he would explain. The villagers thought she might not be married as long as he was alive.

Sometimes, Saroja made me do interesting things like arranging for her bath, and fetching her clothes including her skirt, bra and blouse after her bath. Besides, I was asked to apply oil to her hair. I am afraid, she too treated me like a child. At times, she even undressed in my presence. During nights, if she felt restless, she would call me into her room and ask me to fan her to sleep. I found a variety of books that had nude pictures of men and women lying on her bed. Pretending it to be sultry, she would take her blouse off right before my eyes. When I saw all this, the blood in my veins would course in great fury. I didn't feel like doing anything unless I kept always close to her.

One day, when I came to her room with a cup of coffee in my hand, she was changing her blouse. I stood there staring at her. My watching her undress was not new to either of us. But, now on seeing me there, she became furious. I didn't know what she found in my looks, but she shook with anger. 'Rascal, what are you looking at? Who called you in? Get out, you brute. I thought you are a nice boy. Get out... out,' Saroja shouted at me as if she had gone mad. I immediately came away.

Another funny thing happened the next day.

I was taking bath at the well in the backyard. Saroja came there calling out to me. I had nothing on me expect a loin cloth. She stood looking at me. My body looked hard like granite as I had worked hard and eaten well since my childhood. I don't know what she found in my body, she stood there rooted to the ground for a while and then reluctantly moved away. Since then she religiously kept away from me. She felt irritated by my very presence. She would get angry and call me names — buffalo, donkey and insensitive fellow. She would warn me not to go anywhere near her. But I realized that it was a pleasure to be in her company however much she disliked me. So, I often intentionally confronted her wearing only a lion cloth. She would then get furious and say, 'You beast, why do you roam around like a *bairagi.* If I see you again like this, I'll cut you into pieces.'

Still, I didn't stop going into her presence.

One day, she said to her father, 'We don't need this fellow here anymore, father. Send him back to Ramireddy.'

He laughed at this and said, 'Poor Saru, he looks stupid, but he is loyal. He does everything he is told to do. We won't find another servant like him these days.'

'That may be true, father. Still, I find him unbearable. He can't understand anything. He's been a great nuisance. It's painful to have him around,' she said looking sad.

'Everything here is new to him, isn't it? He'll learn soon. It'll be okay. If we throw him our now, we won't be able to find a servant like him again,' hc said in a conciliatory tone.

Saroja behaved strangely after that. I found her always lost in thought and unmindful of the surroundings. One evening, Reddy was not at home. He went out on one of his 'hunting' trips. It was past ten at night. Saroja called me to her room after a long gap. She was obviously not able to summon sleep and lay tossing on her bed. There was an open book beside her. It was one of the books of nude pictures that she always read. I felt fear creeping into me. With dishevelled hair, body profusely sweating, her face wearing a look of deep anguish and her saree crumpled, Saroja looked terrible and it was the first time that I found her in such a state.

She asked me to come near her. I went. She wanted me to go still closer. I walked timidly towards her. Out of fear that something might happen any moment, my heart-beat fastened. Suddenly, with a flourish of her hand Saroja drew me to her. She hugged me so hard that I felt my bones would be crushed. She bit my cheeks till they bled. She made me breathless by pressing me hard against her breasts. I thought I would die if I stayed there any longer. But she herself pushed me away unexpectedly. I tumbled down the bed.

'You rascal... thief! Why did you come here? Get out... get out,' she shouted. Her eyes glowed like the embers of tamarind wood. For me, it was all like in a dream.

Saroja began to treat me more cruelly after this episode. She intentionally set me very difficult and unnecessary tasks. She ordered me to collect the long neglected garbage at one place in the backyard and set fire to it. The backyard was very large. She threatened to break my bones if I failed to clean it. When I pleaded that it was impossible for me to do it in a day, she said, 'How dare you disobey me!' She then proceeded to report on me to her father. 'He's not carrying out my orders, father. He's learnt to disobey.'

Rangareddy took a thick length of wood and started belabouring me immediately. As I cried out of pain, Saroja giggled and egged him on to beat me more. He thrashed me to the satisfaction of both of them. I couldn't stir out of bed for two days. On the third morning, Saroja came to me.

'Sorry! Were the blows severe? Where did he hit you? Is it painful?' She said sympathetically, as she let her hand pass gently over me. 'I'm a sinner. I got you beaten mercilessly.' She had tears in her eyes.

This kindness and concern of hers were short-lived. She continued with her cruelty towards me. She asked me to fill up an old pit with earth within three days of my recovery. I would have to go without food till I finished the work. True to her word, she starved me for three days. To intensify my suffering, she would bring something delicious and eat it in front of me.

'What a pity! You feel hungry, don't you? Sorry... stop your work. You'll have something to eat now,' she said and gave me some food at last.

I was sleeping as usual outside the bungalow, around midnight, five days after this incident, Saroja came and woke me up.

Reddy was sleeping in the varandah. She took me quietly to the backyard, and from there to a lonely room which was once used by Reddy's forefathers to store farm implements. There was a time in the past, when the amorous young men and women of the village used to enter the room by jumping over the wall for a secret meeting. Reddy had learnt about it, and kept a strict vigil for three nights and succeeded in catching a couple red-handed. He severely punished them in the presence of the elders of the village. None dared to enter the room thereafter. I had believed that Saroja would certainly take me to that room some day. What was happening now was precisely that. We walked silently into the room.

There, in that room, Saroja showed her true colours. She had been hungry for a very long time. She almost devoured me. She appeared to me not a human being. She was like a flame leaping out from the fire of desire. Saroja and I had frequently gone to the room since then. Every such night she would behave as if she would kill me. She played with my body. She took pleasure in torturing me. She wouldn't let me even breathe. I feared I wouldn't be alive if I continued with this liaison any longer. I thought of running away from the house and from Saroja, but I couldn't. I found myself enamoured of her. With her increasing sadism, my pleasure too enhanced.

✡ ✡ ✡

With the dogs, which had fallen silent a short while ago, starting to bark again I was brought back to the present. Reddy, sleeping in the verandah, snored so loudly that he could be heard from quite a distance. Saroja hadn't come yet. She might be sleeping in her room... She might not come tonight. Could I live if she didn't come at all?... What if I went myself into the room to wake her up... But, I was suddenly seized by fear. If Reddy, waking up by chance, found me walking towards her room, he would bury me alive or cut me into pieces with an axe. The bird flew over me again. My hands and legs began to tremble in fear. There was no doubt... I was going to die before the day-break. I felt as if my heart would break, unable to contain the fear.

Suddenly, the door opened with a creak. I was startled — Saroja was walking on tiptoe. She crossed the verandah where her father lay snoring. Nobody in the world could disturb Reddy's sleep! It was an intoxication for him. He wouldn't wake up even if a thousand elephants stepped over him! Saroja came to me, clad in a foam-white saree and blouse. She liked to wear white clothes. It was frightening to see her, dressed in white, and moving towards me that night. I heard that ghosts also wore white clothes. She was not Saroja... she was a ghost! She approached me silently. I pretended to be asleep.

'Eh! Get up... get up quickly,' she said. I got up unwillingly.

'Have you gone to sleep so early?' she asked.

'I have just fallen asleep, madam. Why are you so late tonight?' I enquired.

'I don't know why I am scared tonight. As a matter of fact, I thought of not coming here a all, but couldn't stay back either,' she explained.

Together, we entered the room which seemed to collapse any moment. It was frightening to look at it even by day. It must have been the working of an evil force which made us enter the room that night. As soon as we entered the room, Saroja lay on the straw. Drawing me close to her, she kissed me all over.

'How long will it go on... how long? If my father comes to know of this, he'll kill both of us,' she said apprehensively.

'I too feel scared tonight.'

'Why?... Why are you sacred?' her voice was choked with an inexplicable fear.

'I heard a bird cry before you came. I am scared of the bird's cry.'

'Which bird is it?'

'It's the bird which is thought of as a ghost, a spirit. When it cries, it vomits blood and each drop of the blood causes the death of a person. There will be as many deaths as there are drops of blood.'

Saroja began to shiver. She held me tightly against her

breasts. 'Don't speak any more... I don't want to listen....' she said. For a while, the silence between us was punctuated by only the beating of our hearts. Then, shaking me violently all of a sudden, she said, 'Let's run away from here immediately... somewhere... we can't live here any longer.'

'Where shall we go, madam?' I was conscious of nothing now, except the feel of the warmth of her body.

'I don't mind which place it is... This house appears to be the favourite haunt of demons. I can't explain why, but the sight of my father frightens me,' Saroja said raising her voice a little.

'You're the very apple of your father's eye, aren't you?'

'Chi! His love is morbid and it's good for neither of us. It is this love that scares me. I'm sick of his love. He thinks I'm still a child. He doesn't know what a grown-up woman needs. He wants me to study B.A. and M.A., but my heart is not in studies. In my life I'll never pass B.A. But, unless I graduate, he won't get me married. How long can I repress my burning desires? I can't live with him any longer. Let's escape, go somewhere... immediately... tonight... what do you say?'

She spoke as if she was possessed. A short silence ensued. I was about to tell her that we should elope. Suddenly, we heard the sound of approaching steps. Saroja held me tightly. A moment later, Reddy's voice thundered. We were half dead with fear. Saroja held her breath and hugged me.

'Who's that? Who's there inside? Oh, it has started again... My backyard has become a haven to all the prostitutes of the village... How dare? ... Come out... or I will kill you...,' Reddy said harshly standing a little distance away from the door.

Though frozen with fear, I had a brainwave. Saroja could be saved from the danger of exposure. I understood what he meant by 'it has started again'... He believed that, as in the past, some lovers had come here to meet secretly. I thought he would let me off if I fell at his feet and lied to him that I brought a woman for myself and I might be forgiven. I freed myself from Saroja and came out. Reddy couldn't recognise me in the dark.

'Who are you?' Reddy asked, straining to take a close look at me.

'It's me...your servant,' I replied.

He let out a loud guffaw. 'Oh, you. It's you!... How come you need a woman? I woke up feeling thirsty. I called out to you to fetch me a glass of water. But there was no response from you. I thought you were fast asleep. Then, I heard indistinct voices coming from here... So it is you!... Who's in there? Let me have a look at the slut who agreed to follow you here. You look innocent, but you are a real darkhorse.'

'I've been foolish. It's my first mistake. Forgive me for once. I will never do it again. I bow before you. Let me off this time,' I said and fell at his feet.

'I'll let you go, but I'd like to see your beloved,' he said laughing viciously.

'No, no. You shouldn't. You shouldn't see her. If you see her, she won't be alive. Please go and sleep. Forgive us only once. Flog me to death, if you wish, but don't insist on her coming into your presence.' I wept and hit my head against his feet.

'Why do you cry, you fool? Won't she be alive, if I look at her? If she is so bashful, how come she came with you here, you idiot? Don't you know, it's a practice with me not to allow the women who come to my house to go without satisfying my desire. Only once... you know it well, I've cut down on my 'hunting for women' eversince Saroja came. I'll let you go if only I have a chance to sleep with your beloved,' he said with finality.

When I realized the import of his words, I felt my head reeling. I held his legs more tightly, with all my strength. I kept on pleading with him not to call her out.

'Idiot! Why should you have an objection? Do your think she will always be faithful to you? It's you today, somebody else tomorrow. Why tomorrow? You'll see for yourself how she obeys me right now. What do you say, girl?' Reddy said and walked towards the room. I resisted him by holding on to his feet.

'Let go off my legs, you rascal. Let go... or you'll die. Go away and take rest. I'll see her off. Leave me alone with her,' Reddy said. I didn't leave his feet.

'You won't listen to me, right? Here is what you deserve.' Reddy kicked me hard on the face. I lost my grip. I put a hand to my mouth and felt blood streaming out. I thought I would die. Reddy walked to the door and peeped in, leaving me to writhe in pain. I held my breath as I waited, trying to imagine what was going to happen.

'Who're you, lass? Are you experienced or fresh? Could you find only this fool of an ass? How about me? I'll buy you a costly terylene saree, come on,' Reddy said getting passionate.

Saroja came out with faltering steps. 'Father!' she cried pathetically.

'Saroja! It's you! You, with this fool... with this...' Reddy trailed off. His dismay soon yielded place to terrible fury. He kept on repeating, 'You, with this fool,' as he dragged her by her hair. His whole body shook with unmanageable anger. He mercilessly beat her, kicked her and spat on her. He pulled her along, over the thorns and garbage, as if she were an animal. Surprisingly, Saroja didn't cry. She was still, like a corpse.

I told myself, I should run away immediately. If Reddy saw me again, he would skin me and leave me to die. I stood up and ran. I jumped over the compound wall and fled the village.

"Nippu Ravvalu"
Trans. M. Rajeshwar & E. Satyanarayana

# ABYSMAL DEPTHS

Nuisance. What an awful noise. Seems he alone has a car. What a hideous horn 'Can't you announce your coming like a gentleman, sir?' A.G. Gardiner's 'On the Rules of the Road.' Seems we don't have the habit of forgetting the lessons learnt at school. Perhaps this is how much of the trash remains unforgotten and keeps fidgeting in the mind. Remember to have read someone writing about memory. Umm... yes, it's Malati Chandur in her 'Pramadavanam.' *Andhra Prabha* has now come to be meant for women alone. All the writers in it are women. Perhaps we can knock off a prize by writing with a female pseudonym. But now a days every second man is writing short stories. Remember... read there are 1200 story writers in Andhra Pradesh. Malati Chandur wrote well, however little she wrote. *Champakam Chadapurugulu.* Shows the innate truth in that story. Umm... poor Champakam, a victim of the jealousy of her own kind. What is this? Can't get to my room however long I walk. Why did I come to Koti all the way from the room? For the fun of it.... How difficult it is to keep from coming over here daily. Wonder how a psychoanalyst would analyse this general craze among students to come over here in the evenings. What is the hell of an instinct which drags them here every evening? Another horn. Irritating noise. Curious...the people riding cars appear to be enemies. Why this jealousy over his possession? If you had a car, would you rail against him like this? Why should this malice and avarice make men slaves to themselves? No definite answer. Everything ambiguous. Many have tried to answer, why such serious thought today? If one starts taking things seriously, things become heavy for him. The one there on the poster seems to be Ray's film... *Teen Kanya* at Liberty. Ray seems to be great, though I haven't seen any of his pictures... like so many people find Shakespeare...Shakespeare is great to us though we may not have read a sentence of his. But is he greater than Kalidasa? I wonder. Some fellow called Kalidasa the 'Indian Shakespeare.' Nonsense. An historian has said, had Cleopatra's nose been a little shorter, the whole history of the world would have been different. Ridiculous. Wonder when *Cleopatra* will be released in this wretched country. How damn beautiful Liz must be in that movie. She is said to have appeared nude in it. Burton said, 'It is the most unforgettable experience of my life.' The nasty Indian Censors will cut it off from us. They won't let us see it. The nasty Indian Censors. How many pictures of M.M. and B.B. were victimised by the cruel scissors of Indian Censors. I wish I were a member of the Censor Board.... Umm... how nice it would be to travel to France or Italy to see these pictures... thrilling. Bloody nuisance. The horn again. The noise of rickshaws — Abid Chowk and the books at the pan shop — newspapers. Why see them as though to buy them? A queer thirst for something unknown to us... some hopeful yet unfulfilled desire. Light and shades. The beautiful nudes on the cover page. *Fair Sex*. Provoking. *Hindunation*. Saroja Devi in the news. Be careful, fool, lest someone should catch sight of you here before these dirty, cheap magazines. Wish it were a little nearer so I could read it too. How about buying a copy. Fool, don't you have sense? Haven't got money even for bus fares. Shame. Besides, studying B.A. and still wish to buy these cheap things. Shame. People consider you cultured and civilized. Still, show interest in such scandals as the *Hindunation* would present? How long will you stand here, fool? Look. The shopkeeper already wears a question mark on his face. Get along. Nasty. It's still far away. Wow, the one in the rickhaw is a beauty. Sadhana hair style! It has become popular these days. The American girl, in the bus a few days ago. She too has adopted Sadhana's style. Sadhana is dam-m-mn pretty. 'Mere Jeevan ke dori se bandh liye hum.' Chi... singing aloud has become a habit. Cinema is corrupting young people like us. How nice it would be to have written his essay, 'Cinema is Just a Passive Entertainment'... Russell... poor Russell.... Anxious to save humanity from the scourge of war...scourge...the Charter of the United Nations. What a pity, Russell has been put in jail. Oh, missing. 'Chalo ek bar phir se ajnabi banjaje hum dono.' Stop! 'Chalo ek bar...' Who is that dame in the red sari? Looks like Kumudini. Beautiful college mate...yes, it is she. A beauty. Those charming eyes and the brilliant face, the kind of beauty to stand for beauty contests like Miss College...no, Miss India, even Miss World. An exciting and frustrating beauty. 'Adavari Oorachupulu.' The fellow has changed the record. A dirty song...but it is pretty good to hear. Looks as though all the people are looking at her. 'Adavari Oorachupulu.' Dirty habit. Singing aloud again. Hey, the man coming behind her in the white suit looks like our Political Science Lecturer... Kamalakar Rao. Isn't it strange to see them here! So...the scandal at the college is true. Everyone thought it to be just a rumour all these days. College walls are full of stories about them. Nasty. It's nasty to write like that. 'It's indecent on their part.' Damn it, speaking aloud again... and to myself. Who's written that? But is this what these people are doing....going like that? 'Chalo ek bar phir se.' Phir nahi gana. The same song again... the incessant habit. So, what they talk about in college is true. I was innocent...couldn't believe it. 'What's the time, sir?' Who is this fellow ? It's a sin to have a watch in this country. Everyone asks for time! Foolish. Are you the only one in this world who has a watch? But why should these fellows disturb us? 'Umm... six-thirty — no, six-thirty-three.' Where did I stop? Murli. So, what he has been saying about them is true... all that about them...that these two go to the cinema together, sit in one rickshaw, close together, forgetting themselves in embrace. All true then. But how could that fellow see all this? Six-thirty already, isn't it? How long am I to stand here? The songs are not interesting. Wonder where these two are going! Perhaps they will go to some Public Garden or to Tankbund and happily... 'Entha hayee ee rayee, Entha madhura mee hayi....' So this is what they are doing behind everybody's back. Why do you wail over their happiness? Why, they love each other. Let them do as they like. What do you have to do with it? Jealousy...jealousy! Didn't I feel bad when they wrote all those nasty things? Didn't I argue? But you read all those nasty things with curious, lurid interest, saw with pleasure all those nasty pictures they drew in the johns. Didn't you see them a number of times? All curiosity... what might be the reason for this ugly curiosity? A psychiatrist might help me. Oh, the hell of thinking! Unending stream of thoughts. Damn tiresome. Chalo ekbar phirse ajnabhi banjaye hum dono... Chalo ekbar phirse... Curious, this reverberating. Perhaps this is what hey call a haunting song. Do they sing songs as are sung in the movies? No, they will embrace... closely... closer... closer still... saying... joining lips. Rock Hudson and Ginny. Hell, wretched life.. ours is always like that, a desert, unending. I must tell this everyone at college. Tell that I have seen them going with hands locked tight. All the black-boards will fill with reports of this episode. Murli is terrible. A dangerous fellow, capable of doing anything. This might even appear in *Hindunation*. My God! How harmful it would be to them. I have an evil heart. They haven't done me any harm, after all. Why should I be so malicious towards Kumudini? I don't know... don't know. Can't help it. But is there anything to report here? She might have come this way for shopping and he might have chanced to be here to have a cup of coffee. May be, it is purely accidental to see two people involved in scandal together. Why shouldn't it be taken as an accident? But does it seem like that? There can't be smoke without fire. Why should they talk about it at the college unless there is something between them? Nonsense. Don't worry about all that. Just see, you have been brooding over a great harm to her. Unjust rumour as it is, the whole world will know it. It will be a blot on her character. Who will marry her then? And she will suffer all her life. All this is your imagination... a culture of cinemas and stories. But they can also prove true in life... what if it is true? Still, why should you give publicity to it? Young men like you are pillars of society. And this is why the society is so wretched today. Society...all emotion...it has no specific meaning. No, nothing in this world has a meaning. This life itself has no meaning. Someone said it is a 'story told by an idiot full of sound and fury signifying nothing.' This is the only conclusion for everything that you can think of. Hell of thinking...umm...at last, reached the room. There. Murli is coming. What if I tell him the event of this evening. Nonsense. Are you still undecided... Hamlet...no, don't tell. What if I tell...shouldn't be told...But what if I give it away...Telling? No.

'Hello.'

'Hello, Murli.' No, don't tell... telling it?... No.

'What's the news?'

'Nothing...' Don't... telling? 'You know what happened this evening?' No, fool... don't. Have sense...be careful.

'Yes, what is it?'

What is it...What a curiosity! 'This evening, Kunudini and Kamalakar were going together...holding hands like a newly-wed couple.' All nonsense... false. My God, what an evil heart I have!

'Right-o! Christine Keeler of Arts and Commerce College.'

Made a blunder...weak-willed louse...You are always the same... always the same... the same....

"Adholokam"

Trans. P. Shiv Kumar

# SACRIFICE

Veeraiah became a rich farmer by dint of hard work, careful planning and by sacrificing many little pleasures of life. He could raise practically no crops in the three acres of dry land his father left him. Looking back on his life, he could see how as a boy he was kept in the service of a rich land lord. He never liked to work under this master or anybody else. He took up the cultivation of the little land he inherited, still as a young man. He worked day in and day out but the yield hardly kept the wolf from his door.

About this time a number of changes were introduced in farming. Veeraiah was not slow to benefit from these developments. He carefully studied the high-yielding varieties of seeds and chemical fertilizer by using which his fellow farmers were raising good crops. He wasted little time in pawning the jewellery of his wife and with the capital so raised he bought improved seeds and fertilizer. Rains played fair with him that year and he was able to squeeze gold from his land.

His wife now came forward to share his work. They would spend all their time on their land and their sweat and tears would mix with the earth. When they felt the need to irrigate the land they dug a well, putting their resources to great strain. Now, it was no more jowar or bajra that Veeraiah raised on his land. He went in for commercial crops like chillies and cotton. He could soon make a neat profit on his crops. He promptly repaid all his debts.

His two sons came of age. He withdrew them from school and put them to agriculture. Luck favoured Veeraiah; the three acres of land, adjoining his, came up for sale. Its owner was migrating to city and Veeraiah bought it at the rate of a thousand rupees an acre. To Veeraiah even this barren piece of land yielded gold.

Veeraiah had no bad habits and no wasteful expending on that score. He would often insist that his wife and children too spend less and less. This naturally resulted in greater savings which he invested again, and before long Veeraiah was one of the rich men of the village.

The Land Ceiling Act of the state put the traditionally land-owning class on tenterhooks. One such was Narayan Rao. He decided to sell as much of his land as possible before the Act came into force. This came as a god-send to Veeraiah. He promptly bought ten acres of land which lay on the out-skirts of the village. He even incurred a small debt for the purpose. The dowry his elder son's bride brought about this time had also been of great help.

Now, Veeraiah owned land at two places. It became necessary for him to hire four or five farm hands. He demolished his old hut and built a brand new house. A cattle shed sprang up to accommodate his beasts of burden. He showed some shrewdness in marketing his produce. He would study the prevailing prices at various markets and when the prices were the highest, he would sell his produce.

The attention of the village came to be focussed on Veeraiah. The villagers knew him as a virtual pauper not very long ago. 'Why do you still call yourself *Veeraiah*?' they would say. 'You are Veera Reddy.' Veeraiah belonged to the Kapu community. He knew people were calling him a Reddy because of the popular tradition that when a Kapu becomes rich he would be called a Reddy. He did not like to be called Veera Reddy, but he could not help it. For his sons, however, this new social status was most welcome. They enjoyed every bit of it. They were now called Ram Reddy and Raja Reddy in stead of Ramaiah and Rajaiah. Anybody addressing them Ramaiah and Rajaiah by force of habit was sure to get a sharp disapproving look from them.

The marriage of Raja Reddy followed next. His in-laws gave him a fat dowry. The young couple wanted rich clothes and luxury items. They made frequent trips to the city to watch films. They didn't like to work hard in the fields and so hired more and more workers. The laziness of the young people enraged Veeraiah but he had already grown to be indulgent towards them.

A year ago Veeraiah bought another ten acres of wet land from Bhoopal Reddy, a rich land lord who wanted to migrate to the city. This piece of land lay very close to the village. Veeraiah got a big well dug in it. During summer the villagers came to the well for bathing and washing clothes. Young boys took great pleasure in swimming in the well for hours on end, much to the chagrin of Veeraiah. He would often shout at them and chase them away. One day the patwari's son was caught by Veeraiah. He did not discriminate him in calling names. One of the boys reminded Veeraiah who the boy was, but such was his fury that he paid no attention to the advice.

That evening patwari Narasimha Rao summoned Veeraiah to his house. 'I hear that you called my son names,' said the patwari pointedly.

'They made a cesspool of my well.' Veeraiah didn't bother to pay the usual respect due to the man before him. 'What else do you expect me to do?'

'What will happen to your well if the boys swim for a while?' The patwari was relentless. 'Do you have to call them names? Can't you see, your well happens to be near the village; the kids greatly enjoy a swim now and then. You use obscene language even when you know he is my son. Let me tell you Veeraiah, I am not amused.'

'Whether you are amused or not is your problem, patwari,' Veeraiah snapped. 'They made a mess of my well. My blood boiled and I spoke the way I did.' He turned back and swiftly walked away.

'The pride of riches has gone to his head,' observed

Narasimha Rao. 'He goes giving himself the airs of a zamindar. I think, now he won't listen to anybody.'

About this time the State Government proposed to supply electricity to the village. The sarpanch took the lead in getting power connections to irrigation wells. He asked the farmers willing to get power connection to shell out a thousand rupees per well towards 'expenses.' He roped in Veeraiah too. Veeraiah's response was initially in the negative and for good reasons. There had already been an occasion when he had a serious disagreement with the sarpanch. At the time of Panchayath Election Muralidhar Rao, the present sarpanch, wanted to bring the well-to-do Veeraiah into the election fray. To Muralidhar Rao's suggestion that he should run for ward membership Veeraiah happened to reply, and not very politely, 'I don't want to be a member of the Panchayath Board. I'm just not interested in dirty politics.' Muralidhar Rao came a step down. 'See Veeraiah,' he said almost pleading, 'I've practically run out of funds and there is a lot of election expenditure ahead. Please lend me at least a thousand rupees?'

'I have my own financial problems and they are many. I don't have a single rupee to spare for you,' Veeraiah said curtly closing the subject.

'Let the occasion come,' Muralidhar Rao looked daggers at him and mumbled to himself, 'I'll see the end of your pride.'

Months rolled by. There was no sign of electricity anywhere. Then slowly electric poles began to be erected. Wiring followed. The sarpanch asked the farmers to keep motor pumps, pipes and other paraphernalia ready. He also made it known that whoever now came forward to contribute a thousand rupees could have power connection to his well.

Veeraiah's sons argued a whole night with him and secured his consent. Next day a thousand rupees passed into the hands of the sarpanch. The buying of a motor pump and other equipment followed.

The electricity people were nowhere in sight for many days. Meanwhile a new political awareness seemed to have suddenly seeped into the village. Some young men formed a new party and Sudhakar was made its leader. The walls of the village were filled with graffiti which read: 'Long live revolution,' 'Down with the atrocities of the land lords,' 'Raise the wages of the agricultural labourers,' 'Long live worker-farmer unity,' 'Better die fighting than of hunger,' and 'Power through the barrel of the gun.' Within days a majority of the hot-blooded young men of the village joined the new party and began to actively participate in the village politics.

'Why those thousand rupees for electricity?' demanded Sudhakar. 'Half the money goes into the pockets of the sarpanch.' It didn't stop there. Every movement of the sarpanch was subjected to sharp criticism by the youth leader. He organized a strike of the agricultural labourers at the time of paddy plantation. The land owners had to come down at last and agree to pay wages fixed by the Government. Soon Sudhakar's words gained as much importance as that of the sarpanch. Harijans and agricultural labourers sought his help in solving their disputes and feuds. Things took such a turn that without Sudhakar's knowledge and intervention no problem could be solved and no agreement could take placc among the villagers. He had all the solutions to all the problems, ready-made.

Taking advantage of his privileged position Sudhakar started soliciting a contribution of five thousand rupees from every rich farmer to meet, he said, the expenditure of the convention of his party to be held in Hyderabad. Veeraiah's name came to be included in the list of the contributors. Whoever Sudhakar approached for contribution made it without protest. If the sarpanch, patwari and patel grudged it, they didn't show it. Sudhakar came to Veeraiah's house one morning and solicited five thousand rupees.

'Contribution? Five thousand rupees!' sneered Veeraiah. 'I won't give a single pie. Go, do whatever you like.'

'Everybody has given,' shot back Sudhakar. 'Why don't you too come out with the money. Do you think you have horns on your head?'

'May I ask you, why should I give my hard-earned money to you? Veeraiah retorted. 'Nobody has ever come soliciting monetary contribution from me all these years. What is so special about you and your party? Have you given me any money for safe keeping? Have I robbed anybody to make money? If I am rich today, it's because of the sweat of my brow. Do five thousand rupees grow on the trees? It will not do to threaten this man and that man. Go earn a hundred rupees on your own and you will come to know how difficult it is to earn money.'

'We haven't come to listen to your speech,' said Sudhakar indignantly. 'Don't you see we are trying to help the poor workers and other exploited people. Already, their living conditions have started improving. We have also been resolving their disputes within no time. Can't you spare five thousand rupees for a cause?

'I think I made my intention very clear. So just go away, you understand,' said Veeraiah turning back.

'All right, we are going away for now, but you'll live to regret it,' Sudhakar said angrily. He then asked his friends to follow him out.

'You and your threats! I'm not afraid of the likes of you,' said Veeraiah more to himself. 'I've known you as a child and I've seen you grow. What harm can you reach me?'

Veeraiah's flat refusal to be cowed down by Sudhakar greatly surprised everyone. 'When the sarpanch and patwari themselves are scared stiff of Sudhakar, how dare this man turns him away empty handed,' the villagers whispered to each other. 'His pride will not last long. They'll see to it.' When the sarpanch, patwari and other elders of the village came to know of this they felt it as an insult, not to Sudhakar, but to themselves. They thought Veeraiah wanted to pass for a hero, while they looked like proper cowards to the people of the village.

Veeraiah's wife, sons and daughters-in-law were terrified by this act of his. 'It's very risky to pick a quarrel with them,' said

Ram Reddy. 'They will rob us of everything one fine night. They may even kill us. They are dangerous, these new party people.'

'We can still give them that paltry five thousand, can't we?' begged Raja Reddy.

'Father, if we don't give them the money they will beat us all up into pulp and kill us,' repeated the thoroughly shaken Ram Reddy.

'I'm not afraid of death,' Veeraiah spoke at long last. 'They can have the money only after my death. This is my sweat and blood. I've never known costly clothes, never drank nor enjoyed any other luxury. It's because of my austerity and frugal ways that I see you prosperous today. After all, what crime have I committed to pay penalty? Why should I be scared of them?' His sons knew him too well to insist any more on his parting with the money.

A month or so after this incident the long awaited electricity people came. It was midday when they arrived in the village. Veeraiah's being the nearest well, they started working there. They fixed motor pump and pipes and two of the wire-men gave power connection to the motor set with service wire. By the time they finished this work it was already dark. They left things as they were and went back to the village.

Two Harijan boys were coming that way after tethering the cattle in their shed. They were used to swimming in Veeraiah's well, and there being none in sight, they did not want to lose the pleasure of a swim. 'Arre Yadi,' said one of the boys to the other. 'I feel itchy all over my body. How about swimming in Veeraiah's well?'

'If that man sees, that will be the end of us,' replied Yadaiah to his friend. 'I feel hungry. Let us go home.'

'Oh, Veeraiah will not be coming this way now,' assured Sammaiah. 'He will be enjoying his palm-wine now.' Without further debate the two boys took off their clothes and jumped into the well.

The next minute they began to float on the water, face down and dead.

Next day, early in the morning, news of the deaths spread to the four corners of the village like wild fire. People came in groups to the well. The electricity men could easily understand that the boys were electrocuted. The wiring they did the previous day was defective and electricity freely passed into the water. They did not allow anybody to go near the well till the police arrived. People who thronged the well secretly recollected how Veeraiah swore to offer a man as sacrifice to the well when vexed by the swimmers. The parents of the boys wailed and beat their chests and openly accused Veeraiah of sacrificing the boys to the well. None was willing to believe that the deaths were the result of defective wiring. It pleased them to think that Veeraiah got electricity leaked into the well and thus put the boys to death. Veeraiah was, however, unperturbed even when he came to know of the rumour doing rounds.

The police arrived from Suryapet. High officials of the Electricity Board also came to the village. The Divisional Electricity Engineer made a thorough enquiry and absolved Veeraiah of any wrong-doing. But nobody received the report favourably. They just didn't want to believe that Veeraiah wasn't responsible for whatever had happened. The patwari liked to say, 'Veeraiah had bribed the electricity and the police officials with not less than five thousand rupees.'

'These reports and all that,' the sarpanch joined him. 'Don't I know how much truth there is in them?'

'You've sacrificed two lives to Muthalamma,' fumed Sudhakar. 'I'll see how long you yourself will live.'

Overnight posters appeared on the walls of the village. 'Punish *bada* bourgeois Veera Reddy for sacrificing two lives,' they screamed. 'Condemn the atrocities of zamindars on Harijans,' 'Veera Reddy, compensate the deaths of Sammaiah and Yadaiah.' The wall posters offered great entertainment to many of the villagers who were secretly jealous of Veeraiah. The patwari and sarpanch read them and smiled to themselves in triumph.

Veeraiah didn't allow himself to be disturbed. He went about his work as if nothing had happened. 'Go, drown the whole lot of you,' he shouted at his wife and others who were apprehensive of the consequences and allowed the matter to rest there.

A week passed. It had been a particularly tiresome day for Veeraiah, and he went to bed early. He was in deep slumber when Ram Reddy woke him up around mid-night. 'They say some leaders have come,' he informed his father. 'They have summoned us to the Panchayath Board Office.'

'Which leaders are you talking about?' Veeraiah was genuinely puzzled.

'They belong to Sudhakar's party,' explained Ram Reddy.

Veeraiah was suddenly wide awake. His heart began to thump against his chest. He rose from bed, threw a shawl around his shoulders and came out. Four young men stood outside the door. Two of them belonged to the village but the other two were strangers. Veeraiah and his two sons followed them to the meeting place.

The Panchayath Board Office was at the intersection of four paths, right at the centre of the village. Almost half of the villagers congregated there. The sarpanch, patwari and patel were seated at the centre and the parents of Yadaiah and Sammaiah by their side. At the arrival of Veeraiah a sudden hush reigned. One of the youngmen that brought Veeraiah to the place broke the silence pointing to a man dressed after city fashion, 'That is our leader, Surender.'

Surender stood up on seeing Veeraiah. 'Dear friends,' he bellowed, once again shattering the silence of the night. 'This is open court. You yourselves are the judges here. You all know, Veeraiah has been accused of being responsible for the death of two innocent boys. Now, you decide what punishment or otherwise should be awarded to him.'

'Life for life,' shouted the crowd.

'Does the accused have anything to say in his defence?' Surrender turned to Veeraiah.

Veeraiah said nothing. He felt drained of all his strength. He looked around for a fleeting second before fixing his gaze again on Surender.

'Veeraiah, do you have anything to say?' thundered Sudhakar who positioned himself beside Surender.

After a couple of failed attempts to speak, Veeraiah abruptly said, 'You have become a big leader, haven't you?'

'Veeraiah, mind your language.' Sudhakar felt offended at being addressed disrespectfully.

'One last chance, Veera Reddy,' said Surender impatiently. 'If there is anything on your mind, come out with it. We can't waste our time like this.'

'What have I got to say?' Veeraiah's voice was controlled this time. 'What happened is known to everyone. I got power connection like many others here,' he paused and surveyed the gathering. 'The boys died. I don't know why you think I am responsible for their deaths.'

'Lies, Veeraiah is a liar,' shouted Sudhakar at the top of his voice. 'You have killed the boys, and nobody here has a doubt about it. We know you have sworn to offer young boys as sacrifice to your family goddess Muttalamma. To keep your promise to the deity you bribed the electricians and got power leaked into the well. On the basis of this evidence I charge you with the murder of two boys. Friends, what do you say?' He turned to the crowd, 'Am I right?'

'True, one hundred per cent true,' chorused many youthful voices.

'We have enough evidence to prove the claim,' Surender said. 'Sudhakar, tell the friends what this man had said when you went to the well for bathing last month.'

'Friends,' Sudhakar spoke as though on a cue. 'Sometime back I went with a few friends of mine to the well for bathing. We clearly heard Veera Reddy say: 'I'll offer one of you as sacrifice to Muttalamma. The goddess has been asking me every night in my dream to offer her fresh human blood.'

'Yes, yes...even we heard him say so,' his friends volunteered to support him.

Surender looked around in triumph. 'Now it is proved beyond a shade of doubt that Veera Reddy got the two boys murdered,' he said with the air of a man who had solved a problem. 'Decide yourself how he should be punished.'

'Life for life, blood for blood, that will be natural justice,' the crowd responded in unison.

The patwari, who remained silent all along, got to his feet and said haltingly, 'Poor wretch of an old man. What do we gain by killing him. Get him to suitably pay for the loss of the children. That way their parents will find some solace.'

'What the patwari said is very reasonable,' observed Surender. 'We don't like to kill the criminals when there are others ways of dealing with them. Now, the question is how much should be the amount of compensation.'

'Not less than one lakh rupees in any case,' a youngman came forward to name the figure.

'No, two lakhs,' added another. People suddenly began to discuss. Surender waited for them to stop talking. He then turned to the patwari. 'You know the financial status of Veera Reddy better than anybody else here,' he said. 'We give you the responsibility of fixing the amount.'

The sarpanch, patel, patwari and two of the Panchayath Board members went aside and whispered something to one another. The patwari said, coming back, 'Where can he bring a lakh rupees from? We feel forty thousand is reasonable.'

'Injustice, injustice,' the young men shouted again.

'The patwari has joined hands with Veera Reddy,' Sudhakar declared. 'That is why they beat down the compensation.'

'These village elders are quarrelling with our bread,' a Harijan youth said in great anger.

There was a din again as people began to talk.

'Will you all keep silent for a while,' Surender thundered. 'We must be on our way soon; we haven't got much time to lose.' The crowd fell silent. He then went on, 'After considering various opinions we've come to a conclusion. We feel it reasonable that Veera Reddy should pay fifty thousand rupees to the parents of the boys. Do you all agree with us?'

'Yes, it sounds reasonable enough.' The people sheepishly agreed with him.

'Patwari, draw a document immediately,' ordered Surender. 'Put it on paper that the parents of the boys and Veera Reddy have agreed to his giving fifty thousand rupees in compensation to them. Take his signature as well.'

The patwari drew a document in a surprisingly short time. They brought it to where Veeraiah stood and asked him to sign it.

'I won't realise fifty thousand rupees even if I sell my entire property and myself too.' Veeraiah was blunt and defiant. 'You kill me first and get your document signed by my body.'

'Enough of that,' Surender said starting to get irritated. 'Thank your gods that your life has been spared. If you want to keep your head on your shoulders sign the document immediately.'

Veeraiah's sons forcibly got his thumb impression on the document. The patwari asked his sons also to sign. They meekly obliged.

'Patwari, patel and sarpanch, you too sign the document as witnesses,' ordered Surender.

'We...but why?' the patel objected.

'No arguments. Do what you are told,' said Surender glaring at him.

While the officers of the village were signing the document Surender said addressing the gathering, 'Veera Reddy has to hand over the money to our party worker Sudhakar within a week. He will share the money evenly between the two families. If Veera Reddy does not keep his word or tends to show any cleverness...' he trailed off as the sound of an approaching jeep was heard. The next second, Surender and his followers took to heels with lightning speed. Somebody shouted, 'The police, the police... run away!' People ran helter-skelter. The policemen blew their whistles and fired their guns. In response, they had crude bombs hurled at them. They collared some of the villagers who could not run fast. It all happened in a matter of minutes. There was no trace of Surender or Sudhakar.

There were policemen all over the place by the following morning. When interrogated by them, Veeraiah told what actually had happened, keeping nothing to himself.

The government responded by immediately placing the patel and patwari under suspension for taking part in the open court. A police camp was set up in the village and Veeraiah was assured of all possible protection. People began to speak as they pleased. They were inclined to believe that Veeraiah got a telephone call made to the police while the people's court was in session. When Veeraiah came to know about it he wondered to himself, 'God above alone knows how the police came that night.' His well-wishers advised him to leave the place for a few months fearing reprisal from the party activists. His wife and children too tried a thousand ways. He took no notice of them. 'I've never been afraid of death,' he would say. 'Everyone of us has to die some day or the other. If I have to die, I'll die here in this village. I was born a pauper; I put my faith in this soil and it made me a rich man. It doesn't really make any difference to me if I am alive or dead, staying away from my land. Don't ask me to leave this place again. If they kill me, bury my body in my own land.'

A couple of months passed. Time hung heavily on the hands of Veeraiah and the members of his family. The villagers had been expecting all these days to hear the news of Veeraiah's death. But when no such thing happened, they almost started treating the incident as a sealed book. The police too sensed a marked improvement in the law and order situation and abandoned their camp.

The following night, a little past midnight, Veeraiah's doors were broken open. Four men, armed with daggers, axes and crude fire-arms, burst into the house. They caught Veeraiah by the neck and tied him to a post. Forthwith, they brought their weapons down on him. His wife and sons grovelled and begged for his life, but were rudely pushed aside. The intruders disappeared into the night, leaving the body of Veeraiah in a pool of blood.

Months later it was rumoured that the police were summoned, on the fateful night, by a secret service officer and not by

Veeraiah. While some were struck by remorse, others remained steadfast in their opinion that he deserved death, on way or the other, being an exploiter and people's enemy in the making.

"Bali"<br>Trans. Naveen

# MURDER

Guruvaiah made an effigy. It looked awful with its small eyes, bony limbs and a bulging pouch.

Turning it in his hands, he laughed to his fill. He had made this effigy out of rags and wrapped it up in a colour paper. He then took large pins from his drawer and started pricking the effigy. He enjoyed the activity immensely.

'All these days you did this to me with your abusive language and memos. You thought I am helpless, look here' — saying this he stabbed one more pin into the effigy. He continued this until he ran our of pins.

After a while, he put the effigy down on the floor and rolled it over. 'Ha, ha, ha... see, how the son of a donkey is writhing in pain. It serves him right. He has been a great pain to me. He made me weep all the time. This is the end of you. Today, I will kill you. No, I won't let you die so easily. I will torture you to death. You think I can't take revenge on you!' he went on speaking to the effigy.

Rolling the effigy again on the floor, he kicked it. Kneeling down, he pretended to check its pulse. He then got up suddenly, and cried out, 'He is dead. Our officer is dead. The unbearable torture has led to a heart attack. Now, he must be cremated.'

He emptied a can of kerosene on the effigy and carried it to the backyard. He prepared a pyre with twigs and poured some kerosene on it too. He laid the effigy on the pyre and set fire to it. As the effigy burnt, he stood staring at it.

Suddenly, Guruvaiah began to weep. 'Pity, our officer is dead. I murdered him. He used to scold me at the office everyday. He was always finding fault with my work, so I murdered him. Oh God! What will become of his wife and children?'

He continued his wailing till the flames died down. Afterwards, he went to bed. It was almost midnight. He slept soundly after many days.

✡ ✡ ✡

Guruvaiah was a clerk in the revenue office. He had been a blockhead since his childhood. Always feeling sleepy, he never showed interest in work. When he was just four years old, his mother died. Blaming him for it, people used to speak ill of him.

Guruvaiah's father was a carpenter. His earnings were so meagre that it was difficult for him to buy even one meal a day. He did not want his son to take to carpentry. He wanted to educate him, but Guruvaiah could not learn even the alphabet before he was seven. He slept in the school. Many times, his father gave him hard beatings. Guruvaiah would say to himself, 'If only my father dies, I will be spared.' When he was ten and still in the second standard, his father suddenly died. On learning about his father's death, Guruvaiah felt happy. I wanted my father to die, so he died, Guruvaiah told himself.

A maternal uncle took Guruvaiah to his village and put him to school there. After many attempts, Guruvaiah got through the matriculation examination. He spent three years on average in each class before reaching matriculation. His uncle took pains to get him a clerical job and gave him his only daughter's hand in marriage.

Guruvaiah did nothing at the office. Placing his head on the table, he slept all through the day. He woke up only when someone reminded him of the time for closing the office. He was a stranger to his own files. He took the help of others whenever he was in trouble. Luckily, Guruvaiah had not faced any problems with the officers so far. The officers had all been kind to him. They cared little for the things he did or didn't do in the office. They simply went through the ritual of signing the files and left for their homes. In the beginning, the superintendent of his section used to disturb Guruvaiah's slumber by reminding him of his work. But he gave it up once he realized that it was impossible even for Stalins and Hitlers to make Guruvaiah work.

Unfortunately for Guruvaiah, there had arrived recently a new officer, Mr. Krishnamurthy. Unlike other officers, Krishnamurthy was a serious and work-minded man. A real task master, he could extract work from even a stone. He did not tolerate the inefficiency and sloth of his subordinates.

Krishnamurthy was well-built. He was over six-feet tall. With sharp eyes and a broad-forehead, his face appeared grave. His subordinates were scared stiff of him.

As soon as he had taken charge, he made it clear to all that delay in work and accepting bribes would not to be tolerated. Everyone should work sincerely. 'I will give you every possible benefit but work hard. Don't delay any work. Don't try to avoid your duty. Do your work quickly and get to your homes early. I will never ask you to work overtime. I like efficiency. It goes without saying that I don't tolerate inefficiency and lassitude in you,' said Krishnamurthy to his colleagues during their first formal meeting.

The situation at the office changed dramatically. Krishnamurthy met each clerk personally and encouraged him. He possessed a strange power which inspired everyone.

Krishnamurthy appeared strict and at time even harsh, yet he was a kind-hearted man. Everyone knew it. He talked to all in a friendly manner. He enquired after their domestic problems. He helped whenever they were in need. But he excused no dallying with work. He himself was time-conscious and duty-bound. He worked till the last minute in the office and never went anywhere before that.

On the very first day, Krishnamurthy found Guruvaiah dozing off. He wore a look of surprise on his face. He called Guruvaiah to his chamber.

'If I find you sleeping again in the office, I will see to it that you no longer sleep here. You may enjoy sleep at your home,' warned Krishnamurthy.

Guruvaiah's face was expressionless.

'Have you understood what I said,' the officer stressed his words as he spoke.

Guruvaiah nodded his head in negation.

'That means you shall be sacked — it's all right. Show me your files. I want to have a look at them,' the officer thundered.

Guruvaiah shuddered at this, because he did not know anything of his files. He walked sleepily to his section, picked up some files and brought them to Krishnamurthy. Krishnamurthy was enraged to find them in a bad shape. 'Who gave you this job? I haven't seen a lazier fellow than you in my life. How come you settled down in this section without knowing ABC of your work...?'

Krishnamurthy called the superintendent who informed him, 'Guruvaiah doesn't know his work, sir. We have been indulgent towards him.'

'It won't be tolerated from now onwards. Shift him to the Dispatch Section immediately. Let him work there for sometime,' ordered Krishnamurthy.

Guruvaiah was transferred, but there was no change in his attitude to work. There was no trace of remorse in his dull face.

His sorrows multiplied after the transfer. He found it difficult to dispatch the bundles of letters regularly. There was inordinate delay. One day Krishnamurthy paid a surprise visit to his section. On seeing the pile of letters on the table, he gave him a nice dressing down. He threatened to serve him with dismissal orders if he neglected his work any further.

Guruvaiah made an effort to shake off his sloth. He tried to get involved actively in the work. But it was impossible.

Guruvaiah was caught sleeping once again. This time Krishnamurthy said nothing. He straight away suspended him from work for a whole week.

Guruvaiah felt some disturbance deep in his mind. He remembered the beatings at his father's hands during his childhood. He wished it would be good if Krishnamurthy were died immediately like his father.

In the meantime, something interesting happened.

Detailing the situation arising out of drought in the district, Krishnamurthy himself prepared a special report. He wanted to send it urgently to the Government, and he made on it a special note for its early dispatch. Guruvaiah did not notice it. The report lay hidden under the files for a whole week.

When he got a reminder from the authorities, Krishnamurthy called Guruvaiah and asked, 'Was the report dispatched?'

Guruvaiah said, 'I haven't seen it, sir.'

Krishnamurthy rushed to the dispatch section and searched for the report himself. On discovering it. Krishnamurthy's face went red with anger. 'Rogue, idiot, inefficient fool! I am dismissing you from service this minute. Go away. Never show me your lazy face again,' he shouted shaking with anger.

Guruvaiah did not open his mouth. He was suspended for fifteen days.

Day by day, the desire to see the end of his officer grew intense in Guruvaiah's mind. 'If he does not die, I must murder him,' he told himself. He thought of various methods to finish off Krishnamurthy. He devised an excellent plan at last. It was also easy to execute. This was the plan he put into practice today — to make an effigy of the officer, torture it to death and also perform the funeral rites to it.

After the rites, he felt light in his heart. He had earlier spent many sleepless nights. But tonight he enjoyed a sound sleep. He had a dream too — the police arrested him and took him to the police station. 'You murdered Krishnamurthy, didn't you?' they asked him.

'Yes... I did,' confessed Guruvaiah. They took him to a court. The judge too asked, 'Did you kill Krishnamurthy?' 'Yes,' he said. The judge sentenced him to death.

He was frightened to go to the office the next day. He was afraid that the police would arrest and throw him into jail, but he had a feeling that his crime might not have been known to anyone so soon.

He walked to the office leisurely.

Exactly at ten o'clock, Krishnamurthy arrived. Guruvaiah was shocked. What he was seeing was not Krishnamurthy. It must be a ghost.

He could recall, he himself had murdered Krishnamurthy the previous night. He tried to concentrate on his work. After a while, he heard a sudden commotion in the office.

'What's that? What happened?' Guruvaiah asked an attendant.

'The officer has had a heart attack, sir,' he replied.

Guruvaiah walked slowly to Krishnamurthy's room, while others ran. The room was soon packed with people.

Krishnamurthy was groaning with severe pain. His body was convulsing violently as if someone was driving nails into it. Guruvaiah's eyes shone with happiness. He had a feeling that he had already witnessed this spectacle before and he felt contented with what he saw.

Soon a doctor arrived. After examining Krishnamurthy, he said, 'Take him to hospital immediately.' But Krishnamurthy breathed his last on the way to hospital.

The entire staff were moved to tears. They felt orphaned. Guruvaiah alone was unperturbed. Even the stones show signs of water in them, but no trace of tears could be found in his eyes.

Guruvaiah began to suspect if someone knew about his 'crime.' If they did, they would throttle him on the spot.

Krishnamurthy's body was taken home in a car. Closing the office for the day, the staff too followed the car. Guruvaiah went with them.

On learning about Krishnamurthy's death, his wife became unconscious. His three sons and two daughters threw themselves on his body and wept.

Krishnamurthy's wife was about thirty, but she looked much

younger. She was also pretty. When she regained her consciousness, she wept pathetically. Guruvaiah watched her and the children crying. His heart began to melt. He felt pity for them. He thought he had committed a grave crime. All his colleagues had a high opinion of the officer. They said he was an able and straight-forward administratior. Yes, he was really good. Guruvaiah was a dunderhead and a lazy man, so the officer used to punish him. For such a small thing, should he have to murder him?

Along with others, Guruvaiah stayed at Krishnamurthy's house all the day. After the funeral, he returned home, late in the evening.

✡ ✡ ✡

Guruvaiah felt the police would certainly arrest him, sooner or later. He was waiting for them to come and pick him up. Whenever he heard the sound of a window or door shuttering, or the tapping of footsteps in the courtyard, or the noise of an approaching jeep, he shuddered.

He kept wondering to himself. There, look, the police were coming. They would arrest him. They would hang him. Should he run away from there? No. There was no point in running away. The police would chase him. They would catch him and hang him... It couldn't be escaped. If he died, nobody would shed tears for him, anyway. His wife deserted him long ago. Unable to put up with his laziness, she went her way calling him a worthless man. It was said that she had eloped with someone recently. He had no children. If he were hanged — if he were dead, there was nobody to cry over him.

It was a pity, Krishnamurthy had died so young. People loved him. A large family, solely dependent on him, had been orphaned. Widowhood had been forced on his young wife. Certainly, Guruvaiah made a grave mistake. His own death would make no difference to the world, but the death of a man like Krishnamurthy caused much loss to it. He committed an unforgivable crime.

Eternal sleeper though he was, Guruvaiah could not sleep even during the nights. Every moment, he waited for something to happen to him. At the fall of a fig, he would wake up. On hearing the creak of a door or the shuttering of a window or the sound of a jeep on the road or the tapping of shoes in the neighbouring house, he would tell himself, 'There, they are coming... I must go.' He was fed up with waiting for the police to come. He thought the police were no good. How much time did they need to know of such a small incident as this?

After a long inner struggle, he would have a nap. Soon he would have nightmares. Krishnamurthy, police, courts, lawyers, halter, hangaman — all these appeared to him in their varied forms. He would sit up suddenly in his bed, perspiring all over.

A week went by.

Guruvaiah became thinner and thinner as the days passed. He lost all his appetite for food. He suffered from restlessness and did not feel like doing anything.

One day he took his colleague, Satyanarayana, into confidence and said, 'I have a secret to share with you. Will you come out for a while?'

Satyanarayana looked at Guruvaiah in disbelief. For the last two years they had been sitting side by side in the office, yet they never spoke to each other. Today Satyanarayana was greatly surprised to be asked by Guruvaiah to go out with him.

'Okay. Let's go,' Satyanarayana said rising from his seat.

They went to the canteen and sat at a table in a corner. At that time of the day, the canteen was usually almost empty. Satyanarayana ordered two cups of tea and asked Guruvaiah to tell him the secret.

Guruvaiah began to shiver inside his clothes.

Having had no sleep for days on end, his eyes sank deep into their sockets. His hair was unkempt and hung loose from his head. He had already had ugly looks with a dark face and thick lips. Today he looked uglier than ever. Taking Satyanarayana's hands into his, Guruvaiah whispered, 'I killed our officer, Krishnamurthy... I murdered him.'

For a moment, Satyanarayana started at Guruvaiah in utter disbelief. He could not make out what Guruvaiah was saying.

'You won't believe me, but I murdered him. Nobody knows about it. I did it secretly. The police too have not yet learnt about it.'

'Mr. Guruvaiah! You have not gone mad, I believe. Do you know what you are talking about?' said Satyanarayana.

'What! Am I mad? Why do you think so?' Guruvaiah asked.

'Nobody killed our officer. He died of heart attack. He has had a history of the ailment for a long time. You killed him? Nonsense. It is all right to talk to me like this, but don't say such things anywhere else. You will be sent to a mental hospital. Take care!' Satyanarayana finished his tea and left the place.

Guruvaiah sat there for a long time and pondered. Poor Satyanarayana! Like everyone else he too has been deceived. Fool. He thinks the officer has died of heart attack. All are fools. Nobody takes my word for it.

The restlessness that arose in Guruvaiah soon assumed unmanageable proportions and, like a wild fire, began to consume his being. He experienced severe pain in his heart which he thought was being pierced with thousands of pins. There was an invisible blaze in his mind as if millions of volcanoes erupted there. When he closed his eyes, a halter appeared in manifold colours and in hundreds of thousands of shapes. Food, water and sleep became strange things for him. Waiting for someone to release him from this incessant pain, he had all his energies exhausted.

A fortnight passed since the death of Krishnamurthy.

One night, Guruvaiah got up from his bed and walked, as though in dream, to the police station.

'What do you want?' asked the policemen on duty on seeing him.

'I want to see the sub-inspector,' Guruvaiah said.

The policeman took him to the SI's room.

'Tell me,' said the SI, sizing up Guruvaiah with his eyes.

Guruvaiah's appearance was terrifying. His eyes were red like the embers of a tamarind log. His hair was unkempt. He looked as if he would collapse any minute.

'At least, you must believe what I am going to say, sir. Don't laugh at me and call me mad like the others have been doing,' said Guruvaiah holding the sub-inspector's hands.

The police officer asked him to sit down, and then said, 'What's your problem?'

'I murdered a man. If you don't arrest me, I'll commit suicide.'

The sub-inspector, his drowsiness suddenly gone, sat upright in his chair. 'What? Say it again,' he said leaning forward.

'I... I... murdered my officer, Krishnamurthy, sir. I have been on the run all these days. Since I think it to be good for me to surrender, I have come to you, sir,' said Guruvaiah.

'Where did you murder him?'

'Here sir... in this town.'

'There have been no reports of murder during these past few days in the town.'

'No murders? Did I not murder the Revenue Officer, Krishnamurthy fifteen days ago?'

'Revenue Officer Krishnamurthy? He died of heart attack, didn't he?'

'It is there that you all go wrong, sir. I murdered him with my own hands. I poured kerosene on him and put a match to his pyre. I pity him. He died a horrible death. It is not known to anyone uptill now. People think he has died a natural death. How can you, being a police officer, be unaware of it?'

'Mr... what are you? What is your profession?'

'I am a clerk in the Revenue Office.'

'But, are you all right, mentally, that is?... Is your mind working properly? Or is this a joke?'

'Why do you think so, sir?'

'If you continue to say such things, I'll have to admit you

to a lunatic asylum. Don't you know this is a police station? How dare you try to fool me? You can go now... constable!' the SI shouted. 'Take this man out.'

Guruvaiah slowly walked out of the police station.

✡ ✡ ✡

The sub-inspector was shocked to find Guruvaiah's body hanging to a ceiling fan in his house three days later. Both Satyanarayana and the SI felt separately that if they took Guruvaiah a little seriously, they could have averted this tragedy.

"Hatya"

Trans. E. Satyanarayana

# EXPLOITATION

'Spot valuation is at Rajahmundry this time... from the 14th of this month... I've got my orders. Go and get yours...,' my colleague Mohan said to me when I stepped into the college that morning.

'At Rajahmundry? Very good. I've been cherishing a desire to visit the place for a long time. I'm very happy now, I'm going to realise my dream at least this way,' I replied.

'You have always liked to travel to new places. But for one like me, it's really a nuisance. I find it hard to leave my family behind and eat at hotels for fifteen days. That's okay. I'm going to reserve a berth in the Godavari Express. Do you want me to reserve one for you too?' Mohan asked.

'That'll be very kind of you. Shall I give you the money now?' I enquired.

'Let's think of money later. We are going to be together for fifteen days anyhow,' Mohan said and walked out of the staff room.

Mohan reserved two berths.

On the night of the 13th, we went to Kazipet and boarded the train bound for Rajahmundry. We arrived in Rajahmundry at four in the morning. We hired a rickshaw and searched for a room. All lodges were booked in advance on account of the spot valuation. Lectures were to be seen everywhere. At last, we were able to find a room in a lodge called 'Guest House Lodge.'

The Spot Valuation Camp was set up at a junior college in the town. The college was very close to the railway station. With the bustle of the ever running trains and the smoke and ash emanating from them, the surroundings of the college looked unpleasant. The town's roads too were dirty and littered with garbage. The song — 'Vedamla ghoshinche Godavari/Amara dhamamla Bhashinche Rajamahendry' (the Godavari chants like the Vedas/Rajahmundry shines like the abode of the gods) appeals only in musical terms. When we listen to the song, we tend to imagine that Rajahmundry is really one of the most beautiful places on the earth, but only to be disappointed when we actually see it.

The valuation work was from 11 a.m. to 5 p.m. During the six hours, we had to read thirty answer scripts and award marks. That meant only five scripts should be valued in an hour, at the rate of one script for twelve minutes. A rupee and a half was paid for each paper valued.

We used to be exhausted reading thirty scripts, awarding marks, filling out the award lists and handing them over to the chief examiner. Once back from work, I would go to a hotel to have dinner and retire to bed at about ten. Mohan had a different schedule. Finishing the valuation work as early as possible, he would rush to the lodge and play cards with other lecturers staying at the lodge. Mohan and his friends would gather in one of the rooms, and play cards, enjoying every minute of the game.

I had a tough time, left alone in the room. As the college was busy with the Intermediate classes in the morning, the spot valuation work began only after eleven o'clock. To while away time, I visited a new place every day. Having learnt that a boating trip on the Godavari was a pleasant experience, I went by boat one day to see Bobbarlanaka. The next day, I visited the Godavari station to see the statue of the first Telugu poet Nannaiah, which was installed not long ago. Yet another day, I spent some time watching the vehicles speeding on the rail-cum-road bridge built across the Godavari.

It thus happened that one day I visited the nearby railway station.

A train had just arrived. Many passengers alighted from it and hurried towards the main gate. Just then, a ten-year old boy, pulling himself along on a wheeled plank-cart, cried pathetically, 'Babu, have mercy! I have no legs! Give me alms!'

My attention was soon drawn to him, because he did not look like a beggar. Though handicapped, he looked like a prince. He had a fair complexion, round face and pearl-clear eyes. Whoever met him would be moved to pity and ask himself why this handsome boy was fated to beg. It was this kindness that made the passengers stop and give him alms. Everybody would look at him sympathetically for a while and then drop a few coins into the tin, which he used as a begging bowl. The tin was filled with coins in no time.

I stood there looking at him for a long time. With his curly hair, shapely eyebrows, and sparkling eyes, the boy looked like the work of an artist. He had no legs. He might have been born without legs or lost them in an accident. Squatting on the pushcart, he moved among the passengers with ease.

When the tin got filled with coins, he went out quickly. He pushed his cart hard on the road. Where did he go? I wondered as I stopped at a bookshop to look at the new arrivals.

The boy appeared again fifteen minutes later. The tin was empty now. I understood that he had gone out to hide the money somewhere. Where did he hide it? Did he have anyone he called his — mother, father, sister? I wanted to talk to the boy, but he drove past me. I too left the station for the college, as it was time for work.

I visited the station again the next day. The boy was already there. Everybody took pity on him and gave him whatever he or she could. His tin brimmed with coins in less than an hour. He went out immediately to hide or give the money to someone. He came back again. He seemed to earn about fifty rupees a day. Who took away all his money? Were they spending anything on him? He had no proper clothes on him either.

I felt I should find out the people who had been taking away all his hard-earned money. The next day, I went to the station at nine in the morning. The boy was not there. But when a train arrived, he appeared I don't know from where. He cried, 'Babu,

babu, I've no legs, babu' and went round the station. His tin was full in no time. I watched all this with interest.

Then he was out of the station and moving fast along the road. I followed him. He went as far as three hundred yards and stopped at a tree to the right of the road where a twenty-five-year old woman stood waiting for him. I stopped a few yards away and pretended to read a magazine.

The woman looked like one who had come from a respectable family. She wore expensive clothes. She held a pretty wallet in her hand. When the boy came close to her, she seized the tin from him, emptied its contents into her wallet and gave it back to him, gesturing that he should hurry back to the station again.

'Give me fifty paise...I want to buy an ice-cream,' the boy asked her.

'No, I won't. I won't give you even one paisa. Don't play tricks. Now, hurry back. Go, quick. The train will arrive soon,' she said angrily in reply.

'I won't go unless you give me at least twenty five paise,' the boy said and attempted to move away from her.

'You won't? Don't you?' the woman ran after him. She caught him by his hair and started slapping him vigorously.

The boy cried out, 'Mother, don't beat me....Don't beat me...I'll go.'

'That's the way to pay attention to my words! Now, hurry up,' she let go off his hair.

A train steamed into the station. The boy turned his pushcart and drove off.

I waited there for a while, looking at the woman. Her eyes followed the boy.

I then walked slowly towards the Junior College.

When I reached the Camp, many of my colleagues were already at work. I went to the chief examiner and took my scripts.

Valuation is a tedious job. Many examiners would get tired even before they finished ten scripts. They would often go out to have tea, smoke and gossip. They always tried to finish this job as quickly as possible and return to their rooms. Very few people would read every script carefully and award marks judiciously. Some teachers would assess a student's performance on the basis of reading only the first page of his answer script. Some examiners always gave identical marks to both good and poor answers. Some would think it safe not to give too many or too few marks. Yet others would give indiscriminately. Such teachers, though not many, did a grave injustice to the students.

While I was busy with the civics scripts, Raghavaiah, who sat next to me, was going through the physics scripts. I casually looked at the script he was marking and found several colourful pictures in it. The student had drawn the pictures of flowers indicating their different parts. Then I got a doubt. I tapped Raghavaiah on the shoulder and said, 'What's this Raghavaiah? How come a physics script has pictures of flowers in it?'

'What do you mean? Flowers? How can they be in the physics script?' He flipped through the pages and continued, 'You are right... My God! This isn't a physics paper!... This is a botany script,' he wailed.

All the lecturers put down their pens and looked at him. When they realised what had happened, they burst out laughing.

Raghavaiah had already finished two thirds of the paper assuming it to be a physics one. 'What should I do now? Shouldn't those who assigned code numbers to the scripts have some sense? Why did they keep a botany script among the physics scripts?' he said and approached the chief examiner to complain.

'There's a botany script in the physics bundle, sir.'

'A botany script? It might have been kept there by mistake. Let me take it to the ACO for valuation,' saying this, the chief took the script from Raghavaiah and flipped through its pages. 'What's this? Why did you mark the script?' he said getting confused.

'I mistook it for a physics script,' Raghavaiah replied sheepishly.

'How could you take it for a physics paper? You could have known better if you read even one sentence. This is too much...' the chief said beginning to get worked up.

'Is it not too much to keep a botany script in the physics bundle? Let it pass, sir. Please send it to the ACO for valuation.' Raghavaiah tried hard to appear brash.

'How can I send it to him? You have already marked it,' the chief snapped.

Sridhar, a senior lecturer, intervened and said, 'Let's not complicate the matter further, sir. Score off the marks and send it to the ACO. The botany lecturer will take care of it.'

'No, no. I'll report this matter...,' the chief said looking at Sridhar, but he did not seem to be serious about it.

'If reported, it will result in a big mess. Raghavaiah and ten others, including you, will get into trouble. Send it to the ACO without delay.' Sridhar's argument was incontestable.

Everyone agreed with him. They were all in favour of hushing it up. The chief went out without another word.

'Hello Raghavaiah, be attentive. How will things work if you are so careless in marking the scripts?' Sridhar admonished Raghavaiah.

'I've been careful, but this was an oversight. To tell you the truth, I was thinking of something else then...' Raghavaiah said in explanation.

'Were you thinking of your wife, back home?' Sridhar laughed and all the lecturers joined him with a chorus of guffaws.

Raghavaiah was unabashed. He too laughed with them.

At the end of the day's work, most of the lecturers left the hall. I finished my work and left for my room at four-thirty. When I reached the room, Mohan and his friends were already playing cards.

'What? You have come so early today!' I addressed Mohan.

'We came here at half past three. Do you think we stay there till five everyday like you?' Mohan knit his eyebrows and threw a mischievous glance at me.

When I was preparing to change my dress, Mohan said, 'Keep it on, we are going to see a film today.'

'A film? No, I'm tired.'

'Won't you get tired if you are so deeply involved in work! Let's see a film, so you can feel relaxed for a few hours.'

When the card game came to an end, Mohan's friends rose to go to their rooms. We left for the cinema theatre. Mohan looked very happy. He walked by my side whistling to himself.

'What's the matter? You look happy today,' I couldn't hide my curiosity.

'I won a hundred rupees at the game. Doesn't it make one happy if money comes just like that?'

'Yes, indeed it does.'

'Why have we come here if not to earn an extra thousand. It's a big amount. We don't need to work much to earn it. There are some who can mark thirty scripts within an hour.'

'Has it ever occurred to you that such people do a great disservice to the students? Doesn't it amount to cheating the students? Our students are like our children. How heinous it is to cheat our own children,' I said as emotion built up in me.

'You're needlessly getting worked up, sir. The society in which we live has been founded on exploitative values. Cheating and exploitation are commonplace here. The system doesn't care for higher values. Here, a mother exploits her child and the child the mother... Have we been able to contain all this?'

'All right, that may be true. At least *we* should not be a party to it, even if we aren't able to stop it?'

'Impossible. Everybody, in spite of the best efforts, would get sucked into the system,' Mohan went on explaining the different forms of exploitation until we reached the theatre.

Mohan told me that it was the best theatre in the town. He went to the counter marked, 'Dress Circle' and bought two tickets for us. We entered the air-conditioned cinema hall and for a while it looked like heaven on earth.

The film hadn't begun yet.

A few minutes later two women came in and sat beside us. On looking at them, I felt I saw one of them somewhere. Where did I see her?...Where?...I struggled hard to recollect where I saw her...It then came to my mind in a flash, it was at the railway station: the push cart... the boy without legs...the tin with coins in it....

I shut my eyes tightly. Yes, what Mohan said was right. The exploitative system does not care for highers values!

"Dopidi"

Trans. E. Satyanarayana

# GRUDGE

I have decided to kill my father tonight. I am eagerly waiting for him to return to our hut. It is past ten already.

An owl is hooting menacingly from the branches of the tamarind tree near our hut. In the neighbouring hut, the old man is coughing his lungs out. Far away, in another hut, a baby is bawling. Near the street light pole, two dogs are fighting endlessly, barking at each other. On the main road, a couple of streets away, the honking of a car horn. The whirring of moving rickshaw wheels. The first show cinema seems to have ended. The air is still. I am sweating all over. My younger brother and sister are sleeping next to me. Mother is in hospital.

Come what may, I must kill my father tonight. Until then, my anger will not cool down and my family won't see good days again.

He will be coming in a short while — fully drunk, tripping and mumbling — like a thief. As soon as he comes, he will start searching the pots to see if there is something to eat. Mother used to spare some food for him everyday, after we have all eaten. He would steal into the hut like a thief, guzzle the food, and go off to sleep. Tonight too, I left some food for him. He will eat it and die. The trouble will be gone with that. I added pesticide poison to his food. After I took the decision to kill him, this is what I planned for him. Some of our neighbours raise vegetable crops. They keep pesticides always ready with them. I managed to get a little of the poison by lying to them that we too are growing vegetables and that the crop is plagued by pests. I mixed it with his food. The devil, he will come home hungry, eat the stuff and fall dead. Only then will I rest. Only then will I have peace of mind.

But, shouldn't I tell you why I have decided to kill my father?

My father is a drunkard.

My father is a gambler.

My father is a shameless and feckless fellow.

My father has completely ruined the family.

He steals the money mother and I earn working hard.

He starves us to death. When we object to his stealing our money, he severely beats mother and me.

He is pitiless, cruel. He has a stone heart.

'Unless you die, we won't see good times,' mother would often say.

Mother wanted to educate me. She started working as a maid in several houses. She brought in thirty rupees a month, but the next day father would squander it on drink. No amount of mother's pleading and wailing would be of any avail.

Ours is a very small hut. It is not possible to hide money from father in this hut.

When we were living at our native village, I used to go to school. But, after moving to the city, and understanding the financial status of the family, I felt it was not possible for me to continue attending school. I wanted to somehow help my mother. I learnt rickshaw-pulling with the help of a few rickshaw-brothers of the neighbourhood. They also helped me get a rickshaw. Mother wept inconsolably on seeing me, barely twelve, pulling a rickshaw.

We were a well to do family, mother is fond of saying. My father is the only son of his parents. His father died at his birth. His mother pampered him, showering on him all the love in the world. Eversince childhood, he had whatever he wanted. He got into the habit of drinking even when a child. When guests visited us, it was customary in our families to offer them palm-wine and liquor. Father got habituated to drinking that way. Initially the elders themselves got him to taste wine out of their fondness for him. Father soon got addicted to drinking. He was sent to school, but he never showed much interest in studies. On the pretext of studying, he went to the city. Once in the city, he added gambling to his bad habits. Playing cards and drinking were what he did all day long. His debts mounted. He owed in hundreds to others. His mother believed him to be doing well in studies and sent thousands of rupees, mortgaging lands and borrowing money for the purpose.

After failing the matriculation examination three times, father was back in the village. It was then that he got married. Mother was given in marriage to him on the assumption that he belonged to a rich family. His being the only son was an added attraction. But mother's people had no idea that, by the time of the marriage itself, the family was knee-deep in debts.

Father never knew how to do farming or get work done by farm hands, used as he was to borrowing money and making merry with it. Within five years of mother's joining the family as daughter in law, it went bankrupt. The land was gone, acre after acre, to repay the debts. The house, worth more than five thousand rupees, too was attached by a court to recover loans. On the day of the attachment, my grand mother took to bed. A few days later, she was gone. I can still vividly recall her death.

When I was a little boy, mother would often gather me to her bosom and cry for hours. When mother cried like that, I too would cry. Even at that tender age, I knew who was responsible for mother's crying — it was father. Somehow, the opinion that father is wicked, cruel and an enemy of mother and me settled in my mind. I resolved then that I should protect mother from him and make her happy.

Having lost everything, what was there to do in that village? Somebody advised mother that we could go to the city and eke out a living by doing odd jobs. We learnt that a couple of people from our village were living comfortably in the city by working in rich homes as domestics. It is with their help that we came to the city. It is again with their help that we rented this hut.

Initially father was reluctant to come with us to the city. But, within days, he came and joined us. In the meanwhile, mother found work as a maid in half a dozen homes.

In the city too, father soon found for himself some friends. All these friends belonged to the huts neighbouring ours. That these people should be addicted to drinking and playing cards, being so poor, surprised me endlessly.

Father took to them like a fish takes to water. He would search every nook and corner of the hut and disappear with whatever little change he could lay his hands on. When he found no money in the hut, he borrowed from others. The creditors would come and press mother to repay.

Mother would confront father with a volley of abuse. In response, he would thrash her and, if I objected, a couple of blows would fall on me too.

Many times, we had nothing to eat. My brother and sister would cry for food and then fall asleep. On such occasions, mother used to gather them to her breast and weep for hours. Sometime around midnight, father would return, drunk and singing vulgar songs. On hearing his voice, I used to experience uncontrollable anger. I used to be seized with the thought of tearing him to pieces.

Two years after moving to the city, I started pulling a rickshaw. Our situation improved a little since then. I earned about two rupees a day. But, I never brought the money home. Instead, I would go to the grocer and buy rice and other items of food for the family.

I did something else too. I dug a small pit in the middle of our hut and placed a tin in it. Whenever mother or I could spare some money, we kept it in the tin, and in order not to attract father's attention, we promptly covered it with earth.

Father had no idea of the money. He used to search every inch of the hut. We unequivocally told father's creditors and the keeper of the liquor shop not to entertain his requests. Should they lend him in spite of this, they should better forget about repayment.

After this, father started moving around like a cat that has a burnt leg. He pleaded with mother. He cried. He said he couldn't live without drinking. 'If you can't live, better die,' mother said in reply.

He came to me. He begged me for money. He tried to assure me that he would win at the game of cards and return my money. 'I won't give you even a paisa. You too pull a rickshaw like me,' I advised. 'What kind of family I have been born into! Will I pull a rickshaw?' he swore at me and called me names. He did not spare mother too. He attempted to beat her as usual, but I intervened. 'If one blow lands on her body, I will break your bones,' I told him. As a little child, I used to keep silent when he beat mother. But, eversince I took to pulling rickshaw and started earning money, I became self-confident and sure of myself. I felt I had the courage to resist father if the need arose.

Having had no money to drink or gamble for a number of days, father went mad. He would repeatedly go to mother and cry. He even threatened to hang himself. 'Die then,' mother said matter-of-factly, 'the sooner you die, the better for my children.' On hearing this, father burst out crying. Mother too cried.

✡ ✡ ✡

Today I took my rickshaw and went towards the cinema hall. Before leaving home, I dropped some coins into the tin. It must have come to at least ten rupees — this change collected for the past one month, I told myself. I wanted to draw the money in a couple of days and buy a saree for mother. She hardly has any sarees.

I waited for a long time at the cinema hall hoping to find customers. I saw my brother at a distance running towards me. I ran to receive him.

He was crying....

'Father has broken mother's head,' he informed me. My heart leapt. I sat him in the rickshaw and raced home asking him on the way to explain what had happened.

'Father was not at home. Mother went to the bazaar, telling

us that she would be back soon. Sister was sleeping. Father came from nowhere. He proceeded to search the hut as usual. It seems you did not cover the pit properly when you dropped coins into the tin this morning. Father found out the hiding place. He removed the earth and brought out the tin. I ran to tell mother who was returning just then. We both rushed to the hut. Father tied the money in a piece of cloth by then. 'Keep that money back,' mother shouted. But, father ignored her. She tried to snatch the money away from him, but he pushed her aside. She fell down. Yet, she got up and caught his legs, immobilizing him. Father took a stick lying around and hit her hard on the head twice with it. Mother sustained deep cuts on her head. There was blood all around. Father fled with the money.' He stopped speaking and cried. 'Will mother die, brother?' he asked me sobbing. Tears welled up in my eyes. My heart quivered like a leaf with fear, at the thought of mother's dying.

We reached the hut. Already my neighbours gathered there. I went inside and looked at mother. She was in a pool of blood, unconscious. I had no hope that she would survive. I screamed, 'Amma,' and cried loudly, hugging her. The neighbours pacified me and advised me to rush her to hospital. I put her in the rickshaw and took her to hospital. After admitting her to the hospital and getting her wounds dressed, I returned home.

Right when I saw mother in a pool of blood, I decided to send father to hell. Unless he dies, we shall not be happy. Unless he dies, the *Sani* of my family won't be exorcised.

✡ ✡ ✡

At the police headquarters, the clock struck eleven.

Father will come anytime now. I waited for him with bated breath. The owl in the branches of the tamarind tree continued to hoot. The old man in the adjoining hut continued to cough. The dogs which have been fighting at the electric pole ran away somewhere. Far away, the baby is till bawling.

Father is late tonight. He is usually back by ten. Today, his pocket is full. He must be still at the liquor shop.

I am not at all sorry that I am going to kill father.

It hasn't occurred to me that I am doing something wrong. His dying is very important for our family. Unless he dies, mother, brother, sister and I cannot survive in this world. Isn't it a grave injustice that we four should starve everyday for his sake?

I heard the tapping of footsteps outside the hut and sat up. He is coming. I didn't know why, he was pressing his hands to his stomach. He wasn't able to walk steadily. He was faltering. He must have taken an overdose of liquor, I thought. As he entered the hut, he collapsed to the ground, his hands still pressed to his stomach. I went near him and said harshly, '*Doragaru* seems to have had an overdose today.'

Beating his stomach, he started screaming.

'Yes, I drank... I drank to die.... I'm dying.... Ayyo.... Ammo.' His screams were pitiful. Continuing to hit himself on the stomach, he lay on the ground and writhed in pain, like a cock whose head has been just severed.

I was scared. I thought he would die minute. I felt pity for him.

'What happened, father, what happened?' I asked him holding him firmly.

'Where is your mother?'

'You beat her. She is in hospital.'

'Yes... I beat her... I'm a demon. .. I've been a *Yama* for you all. But, I'm going. You will be rid of the evil. You can be happy at least from now on.'

'What happened, father? You've not told me what happened to you.'

'I took away the money you had hidden.... The liquor shop man took it away in turn but declined to offer me even a drop of the liquid. He said the money would settle my debt. I went crazy. I fought with him. He got me thrashed and thrown into the dustbin by his henchmen.

Father couldn't go on. The pain intensified. He started beating his stomach audibly.

His body went into severe convulsions. He started frothing at the mouth. He began to speak again with great difficulty.

'I drank pesticide poison, Endrine. Here, near our hut... from the vegetable-farmers... I got it. Ammo... the pain... I'm dying... Ammo... Won't you call your mother here, just once?... yes,... she isn't here... I beat her... I killed her... That's why I'm dying. This is the only good thing I've done in my life. Unfortunate me, I'm going... Ammo...' He shouted like a mad man.

On hearing him say, 'I drank Endrine' my body became stiff. The thought that I myself killed him rapidly swept over me. My hands and legs became motionless, as if struck by paralysis. I am a murderer. The police will take me away. I should run away. But my legs sank into the ground. I'm unable to move. I collapsed to the ground. Father is still howling and moaning dreadfully. I can't bring myself round to look at him. The fear of being a murderer started crushing my heart. I felt immense pity for father.

Suddenly, father stopped moaning. He stopped writhing in pain. His hands and legs went cold. It's over. Father is dead. 'Father,' I fell on him with a shriek, and wailed.

"Kasi"<br>Trans. V. Radhika Rani

# PENALTY

'How come there are always so many people at that shop?' asks Raghavulu pretending innocence.

In fact, Raghavulu knows why people gather at that shop, and how even those who do not normally chew *pan* feel like doing so when they look at Saroja. He takes pleasure in pretending that he doesn't know what he indeed knows.

'All of them don't go there for the *pans*, but for Saroja who makes them. She's very attractive like a hen about to lay eggs....But, what's the use? Her youth is being wasted like the moonlight in wilderness,' says Saraiah.

'Why?' asks Raghavulu.

'Her husband died in a lorry accident. Why should we bother about all that...come, let's go. It's time. By now, the old man would have opened the shop,' says Sambaiah.

'You're always in a hurry, Sambaiah! Let's go up to that shop and have the *pan* made,' says Raghavulu.

'You've no sense, Raghavulu. Upendraiah gave you a job in the shop only because of me. It's not even a week since you took up the job....If we are late, he won't yell at you but at me,' says Sambaiah.

'It doesn't matter...Heavens won't fall in a minute,' says Raghavulu as he turns his bicycle towards the *pan* shop.

'Hey you, Raghavulu. You appear to be innocent...it's not even a week since you came to this town and you are trying to show off! If you try any tricks with Saroja, she will give you a sound kick. Beware. I believe, once a rowdy who came to have a *pan* made tried to flirt with her. Do you know what she did?

She added something to the *zarda* that is put in the *pan*. The moment he put it in his mouth and chewed it, his head spun and he fell to the ground. If you try any of your tricks with her...you too will get the same treatment,' says Saraiah.

'Oh, no! Why would I do such a stupid thing? I'll only have a *pan* made and come back, that's all,' says Raghavulu.

'Come away soon. Otherwise I'll have to bear the brunt of the old man's anger.' Sambaiah and Saraiah go away quickly riding their bicycles.

Raghavulu goes and stands in front of Saroja's *pan* shop. By the time he reaches the shop, there are three people there — one for cigarettes, another for *pans* and the third for a soda. Saroja is giving them what they need, one after the other.

Raghavulu is looking at her without blinking an eye lid. When he sees beautiful women, he loses no opportunity to introduce himself to them. For the past one week, he has been observing her every time he went up and down the street. He is new to the town. With the help of Sambaiah, he managed to get a salesman's job in Upendraiah's cloth store.

As soon as the three who have come before him leave, Raghavulu says, 'Please make me a sweet *pan*.'

Without even looking at him, she picks up the betel leaves and begins to apply lime on them.

He feels like striking a conversation with her. At present, he's staying with Saraiah and Sambaiah in their room. When Sambaiah's wife and children join him, he will be asked to find himself another place.

Thinking of this, Raghavulu says, 'Can one find a room for rent anywhere here?'

'Who needs it?' she asks, going about her work briskly.

'It's only for me,' he says, ogling at her.

She may not even be twenty five....She is wearing a white saree and a white blouse. She has tied up her long hair into a bun. There's no *bottu* on her forehead. Youth is brimming in every part of her body. Wheat complexion...a very bright oval face —

sparkling eyes, well-shaped eye brows and nose....Raghavulu feels that her saree is not able to hide her heavy breasts.

'How much rent can you pay?' She asks him as she hands over the *pan*.

Though he had asked her about the room just to spend a few minutes more in her company, now it looks as if he will really find one. He replies, 'I can afford upto fifty rupees,' only because he feels anything less would demean him in front of her.

'Do you have wife and children?' She asks him, examining him closely. He is wearing *pyjamas* and a half shirt. He may be twenty five....She feels that at least outwardly he seems a good man.

'Oh, no! ...I am not even married,' he says, as he puts the *pan* in his mouth, pulls out a packet of Charminar cigarettes from his pocket and lights a cigarette.

'Oh! That means you are going to stay all by yourself. In that case, there's no room, no nothing for you,' she says, as if to suggest that he can now go away.

'I won't be by myself... my sister too will stay with me. Did you think I was a college student to stay alone and do all kinds of things? I just joined Upendraiah's cloth store a week ago as a salesman. At present, I'm staying in my friend's house. You'll be blessed if you let me know some place where I can stay,' he says in a pleading tone.

'Only if you promise to bring your sister to stay with you will I rent you a place. Only yesterday a room became vacant in my house. A rent of fifty rupees. A single room. If you come at one in the afternoon when I go for lunch, I'll show you the room,' she says. He feels he can't be luckier than that.

'Thanks a ton....I'll be grateful to you for ever. I am so thrilled that I can't but get another *pan* made by you. Please make me another sweet *pan*,' he says enthusiastically.

As she is making him the *pan*, a man comes asking for a cigarette. Another comes for *zarda pan*.

She makes another *pan* and wraps it in a paper for Raghavulu and hands it over to him. He pays her for the two *pans* and goes away saying, 'I'll be back exactly at one to see the room.'

✡ ✡ ✡

Raghavulu reaches Saroja's *pan* shop at one sharp. Saroja makes her brother sit at the shop and goes to her small tiled house next to the shop. That is a very old house. The mud compound wall has given way at some places. Some tiles on the roof have fallen off. There are only doors but no windows to the house. There are three rooms in all. Two of the rooms are interconnected. The third is separate. Just the previous day, the family which lived in that room vacated it saying it was too small for them.

As soon as he sees the room, Raghavulu says he likes it very much. He also gives an advance of fifty rupees immediately.

'I'll move in this evening itself...but it will be another five or six days before I can bring my sister. You do know about Upendraiah, don't you? Today, when I was only a little late, he shouted at the top of his voice. Except for Sundays, he doesn't give any holidays. I can go to my village only on Sunday to bring my sister,' says Raghavulu.

Saroja agrees to his request. The moment he goes, she tells her mother, Radhamma, 'I don't know what to make of him, but he seems so naive. When I said the rent was fifty, he gave me an advance without even bargaining a bit. The people who vacated it gave us only twenty five, didn't they? I thought of raising it this time by ten and renting it out for thirty five. Even in my wildest dreams, I never thought I could get fifty rupees for this wretched room.'

'Why do you call this a wretched room? Anything these days is exorbitant. This too!' says Radhamma.

In the afternoon, when Saroja comes home for lunch, her brother sits at the shop. He is twelve. When they admitted him in the school, he didn't do well in his studies. So they asked him to sit in the shop and be of help to his sister. She stays at home till four in the evening, comes back to the shop and remains there till nine at night.

Saroja's father passed away five years ago. He used to work in the soda company in that town and also sell sodas in a cart. They have a house which their father had constructed a long time ago. When he suddenly died of paralysis, Saroja was not yet married.

Saroja's mother, Radhamma looked out for a good match for Saroja with the help of her brother and got her married. Within a year of their marriage, Saroja's husband, who worked as a lorry driver, died in a road accident. Saroja came back to her mother immediately after that. Radhamma's brother advised them to open a *pan* shop and even gave them the capital to start the business. Saroja set up a *pan* shop and started supporting her mother and brother. Saroja, who is innately bright, has not found it a problem to make a profit in the *pan* shop.

Raghavulu packs his bag and baggage and moves into the room that evening itself. From the day he moves into the room, Raghavulu tries to mix with and be close to Saroja and Radhamma.

Whenever he finds an opportunity, he tells Saroja, 'God has done you great injustice. Otherwise, why should you, who should be leading a very happy married life, be in this state?' Whenever he says this, Saroja would keep quiet without uttering a single word.

But whenever he expresses the same to Radhamma, she would say, 'Yes, that's her fate. What can we do about it?'

'If you don't mistake me, can I say something? What does Saroja lack? Isn't she beautiful? Is she so old? Why don't you get her married again? These days such weddings are quite common,' says Raghavulu.

'That's true, son. Everyone says such things but who'll marry her?' says Radhamma.

'Who knows which ant-hill has a snake, Radhamma? For all you know, the man who will come forward to marry Saroja may be moving about in the neighbourhood,' Raghavulu would say.

•

Raghavulu gets ready by nine every morning and goes to the cloth store where he works. He comes back at nine at night. Within ten days of his stay in that house, he is able to create an impression in both Saroja and Radhamma that he is indeed a good man.

The first Sunday after he moved into the house, he tells them that his boss wants him to do some work at the shop and, therefore, it's not possible for him to go to his village and that he would go the following Sunday to bring his sister. Radhamma accepts his explanation.

The following Sunday, Raghavulu sets out for his village.

'Where do you come from?' asks Radhamma.

'It's very close to Warangal. Rayaparti,' says Raghavulu.

'What about your parents?' asks Radhamma.

'My father passed away many years ago. I have a mother and two younger sisters. We were once well-to-do. My father took to drinking and ruined everything. We don't have anything now except a house. My mother runs the family doing manual labour. I passed my tenth, came here hoping to find a job and found one in Upendraiah's cloth store,' says Raghavulu.

'Are your sisters ready to get married?' asks Radhamma.

'Yes...that's her worry. The older one is sixteen. The younger is fourteen....I'll go and get the older one.' Saying this, Raghavulu sets out for his village.

He comes back the next morning at eight.

The moment he enters the house and sees Radhamma and Saroja, he starts crying aloud.

'What's happened, my dear?' Radhamma stops doing her work and rushes to him.

'By the time I reached home, the older girl died of vomitings and diarrhoea.' Saying this, he cries aloud once again.

Radhamma and Saroja feel terribly sorry for him. They try hard to pacify him. They ask him the details of her illness. Raghavulu gets over it after an hour and saying, 'You know about my boss. If I had stayed back in the village mourning my sister's death, he would have fired me from the job. I would have lost even this meagre support,' he leaves for the shop.

Radhamma doesn't let him cook his own food from that day. She starts cooking for him too and brings it to his room and serves him. Initially, Raghavulu feels awkward and says, 'Why do you trouble yourself?' Then he agrees saying, 'Okay...you can give me food but on condition that I pay you an extra fifty rupees. You shouldn't say no.'

Radhamma agrees.

One day Saroja stays back home and lies down saying she isn't feeling well enough. Radhamma tells Saroja something which has been on her mind for a long time.

'The young man seems a good person....I would have been relieved if he had married you. Both of you would have worked hard to lead a happy life,' she says.

'You are crazy. Who would marry a widow? Everybody blamed me saying that my husband died in an accident for having married me. Even if someone comes forward to marry me, our neighbours would scare him away saying that he too would die if he marries me,' says Saroja.

'I can't say why, but I have a feeling that Raghavulu loves you and that he would one day express his wish to marry you. When he proposes to you, don't make a fuss, but accept him straightaway,' says Radhamma.

'We'll think about it when he comes up with it,' says Saroja.

✡ ✡ ✡

Two months pass by.

That day, Raghavulu comes back home from the shop at eleven. Because some people belonging to certain political parties insisted on closing down shops, Upendraiah closed his cloth store at ten thirty itself.

By the time Raghavulu comes back, Saroja too is at home. Radhamma had gone to her home town that morning to see her brother.

'Why are you lying down at this hour of the day,' Raghavulu asks as soon as he enters the house, seeing Saroja lying down on a cot.

'I don't know why but I have a severe headache....I made my brother sit at the shop and came away,' says Saroja.

'If you have a headache, you have to take an Aspro with tea. Wait, I'll go get it.' Saying this, he goes out, not paying attention to Saroja who says, 'Why do you bother? It'll go away by itself in a little while.'

He goes out, buys an Aspro from a shop and has the hotel boy carry tea home. He makes Saroja swallow the tablet and sends back the boy.

'How's it now?' asks Raghavulu.

'I'm alright...it's a bit better now. You too have come back early. Is the shop closed?' says Saroja.

'It seems there's a *bandh* today in Warangal. They've closed all the shops on the main road,' says Raghavulu.

'What's the problem? These *bandhs* all the time,' says Saroja.

'Look, you should have a companion in happiness or in pain. If I hadn't come now, you would have been suffering from the headache. If you don't mistake me, I'll ask you something. Shall I?'

'Please do.'

'It's grave injustice to think that you should remain single because you were once married and lost your husband. When a man who has lost his wife can marry again, why can't a woman who has lost her husband? What do you say?'

'What you say is true...but who will come forward to marry a woman who has lost her husband?'

'I will. If you have no objection, I'll marry you. I'll look after you very well...Since I came to know about you, my heart has been full of compassion for you. I wished that I could undo the injustice done to you and bring happiness back into your life.'

Hearing his words, her heart starts beating with some

inexplicable joy. Some kind of ecstasy overwhelms her. Is he just saying things or will he really marry her?

'You may believe me or not...I love you. I'll sacrifice anything for you. Tell me, do you have any objections to marrying me?' he asks, coming very close to her.

She is unable to say anything immediately. She is unable to speak. Some inexplicable happiness overpowers her. Taking her silence for consent, he puts his hand on her shoulder and is about to turn her around.

She gets up suddenly.

'You speak to my mother. It is not proper to lay hands on me till we get married. I'll get very angry,' she says.

Immediately, he withdraws.

'Please forgive me, Saroja. I rushed to do it out of excitement. As you say, I won't touch you till we get married. Is that alright?' Saying this, he goes out.

After that, Saroja does not see Raghavulu for five days. He would come back some time during the middle of the night and leave very early in the morning.

As soon as Radhamma returns from her brother's, she asks Saroja, 'Why is Raghavulu behaving in such a strange manner? He had left by the time I woke up. Didn't he eat at our place the last four days?'

'No,' says Saroja.

'Why? Did the two of you have a fight?'

'What's there to fight about?'

'Something must have taken place. Did you say anything to him?'

'What would I say?'

'Something has happened. If you don't tell me, who'll you tell it to?'

'He wants to marry me.'

Radhamma's face brightens at once.

'Didn't I tell you? I guessed quite some time ago that he loves you....But what did you tell him?'

'I didn't say a thing. I asked him to speak to you. He laid his hand on me as if we were married already. I chastised him and said that it wouldn't be proper to do such things before marriage.'

'You stupid girl! You've no brains. What's your problem if he lays his hands on you? Why did you hurt him? Who will come forward to marry a wretched widow like you? He wants to marry you because he is naive and good. If you hurt such a person, will he even look at you again? What an awful thing you've done! That's why he went away very early without even speaking to me. I knew you would do this, so I had told you to say yes to him without any fuss if he proposed to you.'

Radhamma goes on in this vein the whole of that day.

'I don't know what kind of things this short tempered girl told him, how she must have insulted him! He may vacate the house and leave in a day or two. I have to stop it. I must get them married and see her once again as a married woman,' Radhamma tells herself.

As soon as he comes back from the shop that night, Radhamma goes to his room.

'What's it, my dear? I believe you've not been seen around for the last four or five days. Did Saroja say something to hurt you?' asks Radhamma.

'She didn't say anything. Only I've been upset...,' says Raghavulu.

'That one is short tempered, my dear. If she has said something, don't take it to heart. I believe you said you would marry her. What more can we ask for? Even before she was twenty, she was unfortunate to become a widow. She should be thrilled at her luck that a well-behaved person like you has offered to marry her. I have no objections to your marrying her. Get married and stay here happily. I'll give away this house to you,' says Radhamma.

'I do want to marry Saroja. But I can't marry immediately because I have a few problems. My sister died just the other day. Grief stricken, my mother has become bed ridden. If my mother comes to know at this point that I've married a widow, she ll die of heart attack. Now that I have a small job, my mother hopes that I will be able to get some dowry, clear my father's loans and also get my younger sister married....Give me a little time. I'll marry Saroja as soon as my sister gets married...if people come to know that I've married a widow nobody will marry my sister. I promise...if you give me some time, I'll definitely marry Saroja,' says Raghavulu.

'That's not a problem...do that. You can marry her after all your problems are solved. Why will we put you in a spot?' says Radhamma.

'If you don't mind, shall I ask you something? As we are anyway going to get married, is it wrong for Saroja to move closely with me?'

'There's nothing wrong, dear. She's a bit cranky. I'll have a word with her....You eat at our place as usual.' Saying this, Radhamma serves him his meal.

That night, before they go to bed, Radhamma has a long chat with Saroja.

'He has promised to marry you. He wants some time. Things are not alright at his place, I believe. When things settle down, he said he'll marry you,' says Radhamma.

Saroja doesn't respond.

'Why are you always angry with him? What's wrong if you move closely with him ?' says Radhamma.

'What do you mean by moving closely with him? Do you want me to behave like a wife?' says Saroja.

'It's difficult to speak to you. You always misinterpret my words. He is ready to marry a woman like you, who has become a widow. With such a person...'

'You don't have to remind me every time that I have become a widow. I haven't begged him to marry me. If he wants to marry me, let him. But I won't tolerate if he tries to act funny before marrying me ' says Saroja.

'What'll you do.

'I'll teach him a lesson.'

'You will never learn in your life time.'

'That doesn't matter. I prefer to remain a widow than to live the life of an immoral woman,' says Saroja.

Two days later, a notorious rowdy of that locality called Narasimham tries to misbehave with Saroja at the *pan* shop. At nine in the night, Narasimham comes completely drunk asking for a *pan*. He tries to drag Saroja by her hand as he takes the *pan* from her. Saroja gives him a resounding slap. Enraged by this, Narasimham starts abusing Saroja and tries to pull the end of her saree. Saroja rushes inside her house. He destroys the whole *pan* shop while hurling the choicest of abuses. Hearing his shouts, all the people around assemble there.

'Does she hit me simply because my hand happens to touch her while taking the *pan*? Who doesn't know about her morality? It doesn't seem to be wrong to keep a man who works in a cloth store in her own house and have fun with him! How come she behaves like a chaste woman and hits me just because my hand touches her accidentally? Right in front of everybody, I will...this woman.'

He keeps repeating the same words even as he creates hell for another half an hour. Only after Radhamma intervenes and implores saying, 'It was a mistake...only she was hasty,' does he go away from there. Not a single person who had gathered there feels it necessary even to ask him why he is abusing her like that. Worse still, some say, 'Just because his hand touched her, does she dare slap such a rowdy? If she has such an ego, why should she run a shop?' Some others say, 'How long can they keep it from the world? It seems they have brought home and kept some guy who works in a cloth store.'

Saroja goes inside the house and lies down for a long time, crying. Every single word of his...his terrible abuses pierce her heart like crowbars. He was able to abuse her like that only because there was no man in the house. The society does not pay heed to the fact that she is leading a virtuous life. It is indeed a grave error to have rented out the house to Raghavulu who has no wife or children. Today she has to settle matters with him one way or the other.

After everything quietens down outside, Radhamma comes in and blames her daughter for everything.

'Why do you get into a fight with that rowdy? If he says something, you shouldn't pay attention to it. Those who have no one to protect them, shouldn't have an ego....The people outside too say it's our fault. They say that people who have such a sense of pride shouldn't run a shop,' says Radhamma.

Raghavulu comes home at ten that night. He says he has eaten elsewhere and does not want dinner.

After everyone goes to bed, Saroja goes to Raghavulu's room and wakes him up.

'How come you are here?' he asks surprised.

'Tell me the truth...be serious. Will you really marry me?' says Saroja.

He is scared by the seriousness in her tone.

'That thing...at this late hour..,' he stammers.

'All that's unnecessary. Tell me the truth. Tell me now. Will you marry me...or not?'

'I will. I definitely will. But I need some time.'

'Why?'

'If I get married to you before my sister's marriage, my mother who is already bed-ridden will die of heart failure. Also, if people know that I have married you no one will marry my sister. So, if you give me time till my sister's marriage....'

'If that's so, please vacate the room tomorrow and go away. Don't be seen here again....'

'Why do you speak so harshly?'

'It seems it was foolish to have allowed you to stay in this room by yourself. People are saying all kinds of things about us in this locality.'

He thinks for a moment.

'Let's do this — we'll get married in a temple tomorrow itself. But, let's keep it a secret for some time. I'll take you to my house soon after my sister's marriage.'

'You don't have to take me to your house. It's enough if people here know you have married me.'

'In that case let's get married tomorrow itself,' says Raghavulu. He tries to lay his hand on her and draw her close to him.

'Wait till tomorrow,' she says trying to wriggle out of his hold.

Though she comes back to her room and lies down, she is unable to sleep throughout that night. Even as she has tried to lead a clean and moral life, the society has branded her, insulted her. The more you are frightened of the society, the more it makes you feel scared of it. She should marry Raghavulu and shut them up. Raghavulu is not a bad sort. She has been observing him for two months. He genuinely loves her. If she rejects him now, she may not get another opportunity of this kind again. Will he deceive her just because they get married secretly at a temple? Where can he go after cheating her? She can get hold of him wherever he goes.

The next day, Raghavulu, Saroja and Radhamma go to the Bhadrakali temple. There, in the presence of the priest, Raghavulu marries Saroja.

From that day onwards, Raghavulu and Saroja lead a married life. That night, Raghavulu satisfies the desire he had suppressed for two months. Not just that night...from that day on, he plays with her body every night. He enjoys such heavenly pleasures which he could not even dream of.

Saroja behaves in such a manner as to make everyone in the locality know that they are married. Seeing the *tali* around her neck and the *bottu* on her forehead, the women in the locality raise their eyebrows. Dumb struck, they say, 'Whatever we guessed has happened.'

After his marriage to Saroja, Raghavulu's monetary position

also improves. He gets good clothes stitched. Once a week, when he says he is going to his village, Saroja gives him fifty or hundred rupees and says, 'Take something for your mother and sister.'

After a visit to his place two months after his marriage, Ragahavulu says they have found a good match for his sister. He tells Saroja that they are demanding a dowry of five thousand rupees, that after a lot of difficulty he has been able to get three thousand from his friends and his boss, that if he has another two thousand he can get his sister married and all their problems will then be solved. All the money she has earned for the last two years from the *pan* shop...Saroja gives Raghavulu a little over two thousand rupees. The day after he takes the money, Raghavulu leaves saying, 'I'll come back a week or ten days after my sister's wedding.'

Raghavulu who left saying that, doesn't come back even after a week. Not even after two weeks. Nobody is suspicious till after two weeks. After three weeks, Saroja sends her brother to Upendraiah's cloth store to enquire about Raghavulu.

The boy comes back and gives them very shocking news.

'I believe he was dismissed from his job a month ago because he had misappropriated some money. It seems, they have also removed Sambaiah, who had recommended Raghavulu, from his job. They say they know nothing about Raghavulu,' says Saroja's brother, Murali.

Then they send Murali to Raghavulu's village. Murali comes back from that village and says, 'It seems there's no one called Raghavulu in that village...the people of the village said that someone must have cheated us.'

It is only then that Saroja realises how cleverly he has deceived her. But she can't do anything to him. She can't trace his whereabouts. She feels disgusted with her own helplessness. Radhamma collapses saying, 'I didn't think that anyone who looked so naive would cheat us so badly.' Radhamma who becomes bed-ridden does not get up from bed after that day. Radhamma's brother, who comes to know of it, comes rushing to their house, abuses both Radhamma and Saroja for being so foolish and goes away.

The people in the street realise how Raghavulu took Saroja for a ride. All those who used to talk about Saroja behind her back now start abusing her on her face.

'One has come and gone...how many more will come?' says an elderly woman who lives next door to Saroja's house.

The number of people who sit at the *pan* shop waiting to insult her increases.

'Can't I give you what Raghavulu has? If you come with me, I'll look after you better than he did?' The number of people who say such things also increases.

Narasimham, who had once misbehaved with her, comes one day dead drunk and holds her hand. He again creates a lot of commotion, saying, 'Come, I'll keep you. I won't leave you in the lurch like Raghavulu. Come....'

Saroja's blood begins to boil with shame and anger. She feels like chopping him into pieces.

But she's a woman...added to that she is a woman without male protection. She is a woman who has been deceived because she yearned for male protection.

Nobody in the street tries to protect her from the rowdy. He abuses and insults her as long as he wants and goes away.

She feels as if she is caught in a prison of knives.

She feels she can no longer stay among people who are torturing her every moment like birds of prey. She must go away somewhere.

Her mother who has taken to bed dies.

Saroja sells the house for ten thousand rupees, takes her brother along and goes in search of a destination she herself is unsure of.

✡ ✡ ✡

Five years pass.

Raghavulu, who has come early in the morning to Gowliguda

area in Hyderabad to buy vegetables, sees a woman selling vegetables in a shop and thinks, 'I don't know who this woman is but she looks exactly like Saroja.' Unsure of whether she is Saroja or not, he comes closer to the shop.

There's no doubt...she is Saroja.

He feels like running away from there at once. But for some reason, he feels his legs are being sucked into the ground. His heart starts beating rapidly. His whole body begins to tremble with fear. He tries to gather all his strength and get away from there. But by then, she notices him. Their eyes meet.

'Please come...please come...why are you going away?'

Thinking that she's not calling out to him, he is about to leave.

'Mr. Raghavulu! I'm speaking to you. Why are you going away like that? Didn't you recognise me?' says Saroja.

'Oh! Is that you, Saroja? I didn't recognise you at all. How are you? Have you left Warangal? How come you are here?' Raghavulu realises he can't escape now.

'Not just Warangal...I've left behind a whole lot of things. Please sit down. I've seen you after a very long time. Shall I order some tea?'' says Saroja, pushing an old stool next to her towards him.

He sits on the stool there. 'Stupid woman! She's speaking without any anger! She seems to have forgotten everything. What should I tell her? I had to go away because of some unforeseen circumstances, not because I wanted to cheat you...I've to tell her something.'

'Karim *bhai*, please send a tasty special tea.' She says calling out to the hotel not too far away.

'You must have thought ill of me. You know what actually happened...,' he's about to say something more.

She is speaking to the people who have come to buy vegetables and giving them what they want.

'Why should we talk about all that now? You wouldn't have done that purposefully. By the time you returned to your village, your mother must have come to know about our marriage and died of heart attack. Your sister's marriage too wouldn't have taken place on account of me. With that, your heart must have been shattered and you might not have wanted to come back to me....,' she says in a very normal manner.

'Yes Saroja, that's exactly how it happened....'

'I know it. Did you think I wouldn't understand even this?' says Saroja handing over the glass of tea Karim has sent.

'What news? How are you? You look as if you have become big...,' says Saroja, observing the expensive clothes he is wearing.

'I am running a cloth store here. How are your mother and brother?' says Raghavulu.

'So, you have a cloth store now. Is it running well? Where's my mother now? She is no more.'

'I'm sorry. Is she dead? Did she fall sick?'

'Let's not talk about all those things now. Come to my house in the evening and we can talk at leisure.'

He can't believe his ears.

Saroja is still beautiful. Her youth intact...that enticing attractiveness hasn't lessened one bit. He remembers those wonderful nights he spent with her. He shouldn't lose one more opportunity to be with her.

'Where's your house, Saroja?' he asks.

'Just here, in this lane, the third house. The green door—that's my house. Come. We'll talk about everything at leisure,' she says.

'By the way, what's your brother doing now?'

'That fellow! He's taken up a small job. He has joined as a peon in a college here.'

'I'll come in the evening then.' Saying this, he is about to get up.

'Having come after so long, how can you go empty-handed? Give me that bag?' Saying this, she takes it away from him and fills it completely with vegetables and hands it back to him.

'Will these be enough? Do you have a large family? How many children do you have?' she asks.

He finds it difficult to answer her.

'Me...do you know that I am married?'

'What's there to know about it? How will you remain unmarried for so long?' says Saroja.

'What a kind hearted person you are, Saroja!' he is moved for a moment.

'Take it easy...is your wife good looking?'

'No. Believe me, she is not, Saroja. Nobody can be as beautiful...and as good as you are.'

'Why do you praise me like that. Won't you come in the evening...my brother too is not in town...,' she says again.

'I will surely come,' he says and moves away from there.

✡ ✡ ✡

Raghavulu comes to Saroja's place at eight that night. He wears a sparkling white *jibba* and *pyjamas*. He keeps a jasmine garland in his pocket.

Saroja comes home after closing down her shop early that day, cooks rice and fish curry, takes a bath, wears one of her better sarees and a blouse and applies powder on her face. As she finishes all this and looks forward to his visit, he comes in.

As soon as he comes, she serves food for both of them.

They sit opposite each other and eat talking about this and that.

'Though I had moved away from you, believe me, Saroja, not a day was spent without thinking of you. You may not believe how often I remembered you...how many times I thought of coming to you and beg for forgiveness...,' he says.

'When have I not believed you...,' she says.

Soon after the meal, he lies down on the bed. 'How long since have I had such a lovely meal! The woman I am married to now is a termagant. I married her as I was greedy to get a lot of money. She looks like a devil....I feel as if I have malarial fever when I lie down next to her. Come, Saroja! When will I get this happiness again...,' he says, reaching out to her.

'She has invited me only to spend the night with me. She has sent her brother away to some other place. A woman is like that...if she loves you, she goes crazy. The more you cheat her, the more she loves you. Between then and now, Saroja has not lost her youth one bit. I'm going to savour all her youth now...I have never enjoyed the kind of pleasure I got those two months after marrying this one.'

'You like sweet *pan*, don't you? Wait, I'll get you one,' she says and goes into a room inside. A minute later, she comes out with a bottle and goes to the bed where he is lying down.

He thinks she has brought him something to drink.

'What's that?' he asks trying to sit up.

'You want to know! It's the penalty for your sin.' Saying this she throws the sulphuric acid from the bottle on to his face.

He twists and turns and cries out in great pain.

His whole face is burnt. His eyes too are scorched.

'O God, I'm dying!' Saying this, he throws himself down on the bed and twirls like a cock whose head has been chopped off.

'You are a demon. You want to play with the life of a woman, don't you? What do you think a woman is? She hates as much as she loves. And she has the vengeance of a cobra! I have been searching for you for five years. I have been able to find now. You wanted to enjoy the pleasure of my beauty again, didn't you? Experience it now! And while experiencing it, remember me for the rest of your life,' she screams like Goddess Kalika Devi.

"Pariharam"
Trans. Alladi Uma and M. Sridhar

# THE FULFILLED DESIRE

*I hate her, I hate her with all my heart and soul. She wants me to buy charcoal... charcoal! She has brought charcoal into my life itself.*

He expected her to bring jasmines into his life. Or coral flowers. He thought she would rain nectar on him and make him forget the world causing a sweet oblivion.... But she has brought charcoal into his life... only charcoal.

'Unless you bring charcoal while returning, I can't cook for the night.' How careless, how arrogant! What recklessness, what scorn... about his earnings, his life, his value in the market.... It was so shameful.... All women are the same: they use men as a means to satisfy their financial needs. If men fail in this duty, they don't hesitate for a minute to heap contempt on them.

Wasn't it the last week of the month? Shouldn't she know that he hadn't any money on him? Why did then she insist on his fetching charcoal from bazaar? How could he buy it? Couldn't she have borrowed it from the next door neighbours and somehow managed for these last two days? But, no — she said she didn't want to ask the neighbours... didn't want to go begging at each door... but *he* should go to someone and importune him for some money, fetch coal and then she would cook.

Her attitude — he had been observing since they got married... her conceit, her recklessness... her contempt for him... Her parents were rich, and so she put on airs of superiority. Proud, because a brother of hers was a Tahsildar. If they were such exclusive people, why did they give her in marriage to him? Couldn't they have found her a prince for a husband? He would have placed her on a pedestal and worshipped her everyday. Clearly, Savitri had regard neither for him nor his profession. That was the reason for her indifference, her disdain. He had not known how to bring down her recklessness and disrespect.

Raja Rao was walking briskly to college from his house involuntarily crumpling the notebook in his hand. On the way, two or three of his students greeted him with a 'Good morning, sir' but he had no patience to respond to them warmly.

When he first saw Savitri, he was inspired by many sweet fantasies. She was indeed a great beauty (he often thought that her beauty was the prime cause of her arrogance). He imagined her to be an angel descended for him from heaven. He felt that he had been waiting for her for aeons. He composed in his mind countless romantic lyrics about his future life with her. He longed for fulfilling the passion and the removal of the grief of separation by getting lost in her, merging with her, for all those months preceding their marriage. Savitri and he, a divine couple, would enjoy life to the very core, he felt and waited.

But after marriage, he had to accept the reality of his situation. He observed that beauty, after all, was not heavenly as he had imagined. His desire for merging his life with hers to reach the peaks of unattainable heights remained a far-fetched dream. In fact, between Savitri and him there were innumerable curtains of separation. Savitri's casual and nonchalant attitude, lost in so many illusory worlds which he could not comprehend, into which she would not grant admittance to him nor would he force his way. Her beauty for some reason had become a mirage for him. Desperately he tried to run after and reach for the unreachable phantom, the mirage, but between that beauty and himself there were endless gorges, deep and impassable. Untouched by him, her beauty was like moonlight wasted in the wilderness.

He tried but hadn't understood her indifference towards him

in the least. What was wrong with him? Wasn't he handsome? He still remembered the aged 'madam' with great looks, who taught him Political Thought at the university often referring to him as 'a very smart boy.' He remembered, too, his classmate Uma casting admiring glances at him at every opportunity. But Savitri, running her fingers through his hair (another unfulfilled dream), looking into his eyes as if enchanted and leaning against his chest, never once said, 'You look great in this suit. The colour agrees with you so well?' On the other hand, whenever he pointed to a saree and said, 'Wear this saree, you will look ravishing,' she would respond by saying, 'I look like a granny in it. What a taste!' Once, when he went shopping, he saw a beautiful young woman haggling over the price of a saree. Savitri, he imagined, would look like his favourite screen goddess in it. He immediately offered five rupees more than the young woman and with great hope of pleasing Savitri, his darling wife, he hurried home. On showing it to her she said to his face, 'What a wretched saree is this? You always waste money on such useless stuff.' He spent the whole night agonising over it. Later he found out that the saree appealed to him because the woman at the shop was beautiful.

Raja Rao pulled out a handkerchief from his pocket and wiped the sweat off his face.

Before he left for the college, did she ask him today, or any day, lovingly, 'How can I bear to be away from you for such a long time? What'll you bring me while returning?' and planted a sweet kiss on his cheek? It was a desire he had cherished in his heart for a long time. At least, on these occasions, had she ever said, 'Here you are, you've forgotten your pen' or, 'You've left behind your almirah keys. Look, you've again forgotten your textbooks. How absent-minded! I don't know how you teach the students... here's the flask of milk. Don't forget to take it in the afternoon. You don't know how to look after yourself. No better than a child' (he liked being treated that way — till the other day his mother used to call him a child). Even when she was leaving for her parents' had she ever said, 'Look after yourself. Hotel food doesn't agree with you. Perhaps, you'd be emaciated by the time I return,' or, 'Won't I return soon? Can I breathe a moment away from you?' Should this also remain one of the unfulfilled desires of him? Could such things be discussed with others? After she had gone, he would wait for her letter... He liked writing and receiving letters. At the college, between classes, he dreamt of exchanging letters with his wife. But Savitri wouldn't write any. In the beginning, he used to write long and passionate letters, only to draw from her depressing words: 'I can't understand your effusions.' Once he saw her throwing away his letters along with waste paper. It greatly distressed him. He soon realised that he had married a beautiful beast. He was angry and disgusted with her. He wouldn't remonstrate with her so he smothered the raging fires in his heart. If he protested, she might make a scene. She was adept at passing taunting remarks. One word would lead to another. He disliked screaming and shouting at each other. Such acrimonious exchange of words between wife and husband was uncivilised, boorish. Whenever he so much as raised his voice she would counter him by saying, 'Isn't there a difference between us and the coarse masses?' (implying that she had married an unrefined fellow). He tried many times to adjust to her behaviour and resign himself to his situation. Telling himself that his sentiments were foolish and his desires crazy, he struggled within himself to defuse them.

Eversince he started reading Chalam's novels he developed profound respect for women. He desired with all his heart that women should be emancipated and believed that they had been suppressed and ill-treated for ages in the name of customs and traditions. He argued with his friends about the injustice done to women till he went hoarse. He still recalled Ramayya who used to beat his wife everyday, as one would a beast. The neighbours, himself included, used to watch his beating, treating it as a source of entertainment. Nobody ever intervened and stopped Ramayya from inflicting such cruelty on the poor woman. Ramayya was sure to say if anyone dared interfere, 'She is my wife. I'll beat her and kill her. What business is it of yours?' The woman used to bear the beatings, screaming at him. Yet people used to say that she was of questionable character. To him it looked inhuman, brutal, and his nerves moaned in pain. Ramayya appeared to him a monster, a cannibal.

One day an intriguing thing happened. Savitri and he were going to the cinema by rickshaw. While they were passing the vegetable market, he said just to tease her. 'See the young thing selling vegetables over there? Isn't she ravishing?'

'Where?' she said. 'I can't see her.'

'There,' he pointed a finger at the girl. 'The third shop from the left. I always buy vegetables there. I like her.'

'Oh, yes,' she was flushed with anger. 'Men can do anything and get away with it. If a woman does such things...' she broke off in mid sentence, reproachfully. He felt her accusation hitting him more severely than it would anybody else, because he genuinely wished for the liberation of women. He hastened to add, 'No, no, Savitri. What I mean is, you may like some men just as I like some women. I detest these prudish notions about purity.'

'Rubbish, all this talk of yours. If we women express our true feelings, will you tolerate them?' she asked.

Her question challenged the convictions he had held for a long time. 'Don't you believe my words?' he said. 'If you like any man, tell me now... I won't misunderstand. Believe me Savitri, tell me now.'

'Can you see the rickshaw-walla, passing us by?' she said with an impish grin, 'I like him.' He tried to laugh it off, treating it as a joke. Without his knowledge, jealousy crept into him but he immediately dismissed it. He tried to forget it, yet he wondered how the rickshaw-walla looked.

Whatever methods and tricks he tried, he couldn't come close to her: the curtains between them remained ever intact. One whole year after their marriage, Savitri remained a puzzle to him and her beauty still a mirage. Many nights she obliged him to go to bed without touching her, without easing the tension he felt in his young nerves. Last night, yes, last night, what had happened? It really drove him mad.

Yesterday was a happy day for him. During the staff meeting, the principal said about him, 'A nice boy, Raja Rao. He is doing a marvellous job of teaching, being so young at that.' During the classes he was at his best, sometimes making jokes at which the students burst out laughing. Sujatha, the class beauty who always looked glum, too giggled and joined the others in laughing. He liked Sujatha and he felt happy at her response. He returned home in that happy mood. He found Savitri wearing a diaphanous creamy white saree, which he madly liked, and plenty of jasmines in her hair (he had been crazy about them too) and she looked divine. He regaled her by recounting how the principal appreciated his work and how even the normally sullen Sujatha reacted to his jokes in the class. He felt for the first time that he had succeeded in driving off her habitual moroseness and standoffishness. It soon grew dark. In her white saree and with the jasmines smiling in her hair, Savitri appeared to rival the moon in her brightness. He felt like roaming about in the moonlit night, like a divine couple, exchanging sweet-nothings with her. He wanted to plunge into her heart and probe it to unravel the mystique that it was.

'Let's sleep in the backyard tonight,' he suggested.

'That would be ridiculous. The people next door might find us out.'

'How does it matter? More than five thousand people watched us getting ritually married.'

'Just because we are married, should we sleep in the street?'

'Don't disappoint me, Savitri. Just this one night, please. The moonlight is driving me to ecstasy. With you lying by my side in that moonlight, it'll be heaven...' He couldn't go on. Sometimes he felt he was scared of her.

'Will you stop? The neighbours may hear you.'

'Please, Savitri, please. Only this night,' he implored. Savitri consented and his heart overflowed with love for her. He thought he had not understood her all these months and that was foolish of him. He felt she was a goddess who walked into his life.

Savitri carried a cot to the backyard and set it down where the moonlight fell. They lay down on the bed and he imagined them to be a divine couple. For quite some time Savitri was worried about being watched by the neighbours. Setting her fears to rest and imitating Sean Connory in a recent Bond movie he said, 'If anyone dares look at us, I'll shoot him dead.' He wanted to tell her about all the sweet fantasies that often stirred in the innermost realms of his being. 'How do you feel when the moonlight touches you, Saroo?' he asked. He always wanted to address her as Saroo, but whenever he did so she would say, 'I hate it. Call me Savitri.' But now she didn't object and he felt elated.

'What's there in it. Moonlight is a common physical phenomenon,' Savitri said.

'Is that all? Poor Saroo, this sweet moonlight is sent to us by some kind angel. How can it be mere physical phenomenon? I think it's because of familiarity that the exquisite things of nature appear commonplace.'

'I can't understand such things. You speak strangely. Much of it makes no sense to me.'

'Nothing so deep or profound. Watching the lovely things of nature makes me forget myself. Sunrise and sunset, clouds pregnant with rainwater and the pouring moonlight enrapture me and transport me to the other worlds. I discern realms of enchantment. While I am lost in such a fantasy, I crave for your company. I long to merge into you, to dwell in your heart. In a word, to be united with you for ever.' Looking at the moonlit heavens he was pouring out his heart. He turned to Savitri and grew suspicious — she was not listening to him at all. He felt deeply hurt. It was as if a drop of poison was placed in a jar of nectar. 'Savitri, Savitri,' he called out loudly and in pain. 'Are you asleep?'

'Why do you shout? I just closed my eyes, waiting for your discourse to end.'

He felt bitter. How insouciant! What arrogance.... 'Do you think I have been giving a discourse as I would to a class of students?' he asked her deeply hurt. His eyes filled with tears and his voice was choked with emotion and hurt. 'I'm sorry for vexing you,' he managed to say.

'I told you many times, all this gushing enthusiasm and childish prattle is not to my taste. Still you go on speaking this way. Ohh, I already feel sleepy.'

He felt as if a red-hot iron was driven into his heart... Savitri wasn't a woman, she was a block of stone. He shook with anger. He feared if a disaster would engulf him the next minute. Still he instantaneously took a strong decision, a decision which he had never considered. He was mysteriously reminded of Ramayya. Would he too batter his wife? What would this beautiful beast do if she were beaten up, if those sweet lips were bitten till they bled? What would she do if the jasmines in the knot of her hair were pulled away and crumpled and then she herself dragged by the hair? If he slapped her tender cheeks till they reddened and looked ugly, what would she do? The blouse, clinging closely to her body, if he ripped it and shredded it and yanked the bra out and, devilishly, like a vampire, sucked her blood and romped around, how would she respond? The saree, which was spewing out foam-white moonlight, the item of clothing he liked most, if he tore it into pieces, disrobing her, humiliating her, exposing the beauty that she kept beyond his reach and let out a spiteful guffaw — how would she react? He wanted to know all this that minute. Strangling her, as Joseph Cotton smothers Marilyn Monroe in *Niagara*, he felt like doing it. That very moment he had the urge to kill her, but remained stupefied, like one drugged and incapacitated. A supreme effort checked him and brought the onrushing, frightful emotions under control.

Raja Rao often hated himself for his inability to do what he fervently wished to do, always being hindered by some irksome considerations. Had he done the things he wanted to do last night, how would she have reacted? Would she have struggled? Screamed? What would have happened to her recklessness, her utter lack of regard for his feelings? Suddenly reminded of

Ramayya's wife, he wanted Savitri to cry helplessly like her. If any neighbour objected, he would yell, like Ramayya, 'She is my wife. I'll beat her, I'll kill her. Don't you dare interfere in my family affairs. Is that clear?' Ramayya appeared a gentleman at that moment. Doubtless, Ramayya did what was absolutely right.

Raja Rao stepped into the college campus perspiring all over. He wiped himself on a handkerchief and walked into the office room to sign the attendance register. He brought a forced smile onto his lips when students greeted him. He quickly went to the staff room and sat at his table. Raghupathi who taught economics and Sridhar, a lecturer in history, were already in their seats preparing to teach. Raja Rao had to take the next hour for the final year class. He told the students the previous day that he would begin Hegel and that needed hours of preparation. He thought he would sit with the book at home, but was there a moment's peace there? He opened the textbook but could not do any reading. Raghupathi, sitting opposite him, brought to his mind the need to ask him for a loan. *Unless you bring charcoal while returning, I can't cook for the night.* Coal... the very thought of it filled him with disgust. She would always ask him to bring coal, never jasmines or amaranths. It was always, 'Fetch coal' — life had turned into coal. He had already read a whole paragraph without understanding a word of it. Blast this foolish abstract philosophy! Couldn't it have been a little easy to understand? Damn it, damn everything.

He had a number of absurd sentiments which became a part of his being, got mixed with his blood, even while he was still at college. The illusion that life was pleasant like jasmines and coral flowers hadn't left him. It was painful for him to gradually realise that life was coal, black and unpleasant. *These romantic outpourings, this meaningless drivel, I don't like at all and I told you so on countless occasions....* Yes, that was true, but did he learn anything from it? He had not been able to shake off any of his sentiments. He used to think that women entertained such thoughts more readily than men. But Savitri, the beautiful unfeeling block of stone, was without any. Always pouring over crime thrillers, how would she understand his tender and delicate feelings? He had told her many times not to read such rubbish. He brought home novels of Chalam and Sarat Babu from the college library and asked her to read them. He liked the heroines of Sarat. He had dreamt his future wife would be like one of them — sensitive, tender, loving and caring. He confided in her his feelings hoping her to sensitize herself and match his expectations. But she had disappointed him, terribly. Savitri, Savitri... she hadn't gone out of his mind even for a minute since morning. Hegel, philosopher Hegel... could he understand anything of him in such a frame of mind? With the fires raging in the heart, a storm brewing in the mind? The mind stuffed with charcoal? Charcoal... no food for the night unless he brought home charcoal. 'Have you married me only to starve me?' she would ask him brusquely.

The bell rang signalling the beginning of his class, but he hadn't prepared anything to take the class. The prospect of taking a class without adequate preparation, that too the final year class, gave him a creepy feeling. Being final year students they were studious and haughty. A small mistake on the part of the teacher and it would be boos and catcalls. The newly appointed lecturer in English was treated to them the other day, it was said. That was why the class gave him a fright. Sarala, the most intelligent of the lot, kept the teachers on tenterhooks with her probing questions. Today too she would ask questions and when he failed to give satisfactory replies he would be heckled and jeered at. Savitri was making life miserable for him even at the college. Savitri, what a bother! With the attendance register in a hand, he walked into the classroom and marked attendance in it. Perspiration appeared all over his body and lightly dampened his shirt. A shiver ran down his spine. Nobody ever said that he lectured badly. But today he was going to disgrace himself. With his heart thumping against his chest and sweet streaming down his body he closed the attendance register. He should say something now. He hit upon an idea just in time.

'Let's discuss some general topics,' he began.

'You said you'd begin Hegel today, sir.' It was Sarala.

'Yes, of course, but...' he mumbled.

'Of course...but I haven't done enough preparation —' some backbencher mimicked him. Sniggers (Sarala included). He felt an unbearable pang. Oh, the humiliation!

'Talk sense — well, then, I'll start Hegel,' he declared with a bravado which surprised him. The boys and girls fell silent. For forty minutes he spoke some meaningless twaddle, faltering and struggling for the right words and often repeating himself. He felt his own words nauseating. The forty-minute lecture was a harrowing experience for him. Never before was his lecture so insipid, stale and unappealing. Noticing the students deliberately yawning, whispering and tittering among themselves, he felt helpless and exasperated. On top of it Sarala, his favourite student, was looking at him with pitying eyes. When the bell went off, he hurried out of the classroom, relieved that the ordeal was over. But he could clearly hear from behind, the students commenting, 'Professor has come unprepared to the class.' He felt his temperature rising. Hatred gushed out of his heart for the students, the college, his job and Political Science, the subject he taught. The euphoria generated by the principal's commendation of his work the day before was set at rest by this humiliating experience. These students... such an ungrateful, bloodthirsty lot! Should they create a furore over his one single failure? Savitri, yes, she was responsible for all this, causing a commotion in his mind and robbing him of his mental peace. He returned to the staff room.

He felt as if the whole world was laughing at him. If he went home without a sack of charcoal Savitri would ask, 'Do you want me to go to bed on an empty stomach? Is this why you've married me? I'm not your slave to silently suffer the pangs of hunger. I'm leaving for my parents.' And after returning to her parents she would look for a rich man and elope with him. Then people would hound him and say nasty things about him: 'Look, look! That's the man whose wife has deserted; the effeminate fellow who could not control his wife.' They would peck at him like eagles, vultures. And, after defacing the walls with graffiti ridiculing him, the students would pursue him, yelping and howling. Could he bear that torment, that agony of the lacerated heart... the agony of the twisted guts? No. He couldn't sit there any longer... He should run away from it all. Would Savitri, when he went home, gather him to her bosom, lay him down in her lap and console him and make him forget the world and its problems? No. She would say, in stead, 'Have you brought charcoal?' If he replied in the negative, she would say, 'Then, get out of here. Why have you married me if you can't look after me well?' Her words would be sharp, cruel, derisive and insulting, he was sure of it. She would, like the unfeeling students, like the cruel members of public, peck at him like an eagle, like a vulture and then, in a huff, she would walk out on him, elope with someone. But would she, his Savitri, would she really elope with someone? What a nasty, nasty thought! When the mind is poisoned, such nasty thoughts well up. Still Savitri was wringing his heart, strangling and suffocating him to death. She would surely deliver him into the hands of Yama, the god of death. Involuntarily hc clenched his fists.

Ah, yes, he suddenly remembered to ask Raghupathi for a loan. Would he give? It was said Raghupathi had a lot of money to spare while he was always running short of it. Spending lavishly when there was money on hand and regretting later had become a habit with him. He had never asked Raghupathi for a loan before. But now he would have to borrow ten rupees, buy charcoal and throw it in her face. He wondered how her face would look if he really did it — blackened, ugly, the pride in her beauty gone. But would Raghupathi favour him with a loan? He always felt distressed whenever somebody refused him a loan. He went over it again and again throughout the day with increasing bitterness. But Raghupathi should be surely able to lend him ten rupees. He couldn't say no to him. He held him in respect.

Raja Rao mustered up his courage and said, 'Mr. Raghupathi, could you spare me ten rupees?' Yes, the words were out. A minute's silence ensued. His heart beat wildly. What would Raghupathi say? An outright no?

'I'm sorry, sir. I haven't any money on me now. Sorry,' Raghupathi said.

Blood drained from Raja Rao's face. 'It's all right,' he mumbled.

'But why do you need a loan?' Raghupathi asked, producing a smile on his lips. 'You are just two, you and your wife. You could in fact put by some money and perhaps even lend people like me who have many children.'

'Last week of the month, you see. Harding up a little,' he said unenthusiastically.

'Reckless in the first week and borrowing in the last, is that good for you? You plan your finances properly and put aside enough for the last week too,' Raghupathi was going on and on.

Raja Rao lost all interest in his words. If he couldn't lend, what business did he have to preach him? He despised being sermonized to. It was foolish of him to have approached Raghupathi for a loan in the first place. Presently he said, 'Yes, I know all that.' He rose to go. He didn't feel like sitting there, facing Raghupathi. Blast his advice! Who needed it? Did he mean that he didn't know how to manage his finances. How very conceited! How insultingly did he speak! Surely he was jealous of him because within a year of joining service he rose in the esteem of the students while Raghupathi, even after ten years of teaching, was regularly jeered at by the students on every possible occasion. On top of it the principal said kind words about him the previous day, yes, that was hard for Raghupathi to swallow. He had money, all right. It was just that he was deliberately refusing to lend him any, just to insult him, snub him. Chi, chi, the whole day had been spent being humiliated and insulted. Savitri was the cause of all this! Couldn't she manage for a couple of days without charcoal? Why should she issue such ultimatums?

Raja Rao was walking back home. Strange, that he should be returning home so early, just past 3 o'clock. He should be normally going home at four. What would he do, going home so early? How would he face her? She would confront him by asking, 'Where is charcoal?' He would reply, 'Couldn't bring any.' She would retort, 'What's your life for? For your kind of life, do you need a wife and home? My parents have made a blunder in choosing you as my husband.' Could he hear such unfair remarks, already dazed as he was with the day's developments — humbled in the class-room and insulted by Raghupathi — all because of Savitri, who once he imagined would lay him down on the eiderdown of jasmines, relieve him from the mundane thoughts and cares and offer him nectar at the fount of her lips. But she had been subjecting him to unbearable agony. What was his sin? Did he deserve such cruel treatment? Didn't he have a right to live happily like others? Savitri whom he thought of as an angel had turned out to be a devil... how to face the devil now? He was mortally afraid of her arrogance. Many times he thought of getting rid of his fears and reflected on the ways of crushing her insolence, but always he had been slighted and humbled.

He had believed that his students respected him. But today it was proved that they had nothing but contempt for him. How they laughed at him! He thought his colleague Raghupathi had high regard for him, but today it was established that he had only jealousy and hatred for him. Nobody respected him. When his legally wedded wife herself had no respect for him, wasn't it foolish to expect it from others? She always treated him like a loathsome insect, maybe she even thought him to be mad. Sooner or later, she would walk out on him and run away with a moneyed bastard. Again, that horrid thought of the morning! But she might as well consider the possibility than to live with a crazy fellow like him. As a boy, living in the village, he knew how Somayya's wife Nagi eloped, simply disappeared one night. Thev said Somayya was naive, worthless and that was why Nagi dumped him. Perhaps they would say similar things about him too. Would she really elope — he ground his teeth — would she go away like Nagi? He would then kill her, finish her off. Perhaps she hadn't thought much of him, but now he would show her what he really was.

Raja Rao walked briskly. Just a furlong more to go. What could she be doing? She might be reading some whodunit stuff or attending to her beauty with great care — for whose sake? Not for him, certainly. Then for whose sake? Did she ever say that she put on anything for his sake? Did she ever wear his favourite jasmines on her own? Did she ever say, 'Oh darling, I love you?' Mirage, illusion. Savitri herself was an illusion. He was foolishly, deliriously running after the mirage. While he ran after her, she was probably laughing to herself. Who was she decking herself for, if not for him? Who knew? There might be someone he had not known. Mean thoughts again! The day belonged to mean thoughts. He walked faster. As soon as he stepped into the house she would ask, 'Where is charcoal?' with mockery writ on her face, like the mistress of a house taking a servant boy to task. Now this was foolish. He was again showing signs of weakness. He was allowing Savitri to ride roughshod over his feelings. Why should he be scared of her? Why not he yell and shout at her? His refinement, good breeding and culture coupled with a respect for women, yes, these were the things which held his hand back. But all these were foolish notions, which he formed to hide his worthlessness.

He could now clearly see his house. A rickshaw stood outside and Savitri was talking to the rickshaw-walla. A thought flashed in his mind. Yes, once Savitri did say that she liked the rickshaw-walla. He felt he had at last unravelled a recondite mystery. He walked very fast now. He could see them both: he was dark, stumpy and muscular like a statue of black granite. Could he win if he were required to challenge the man for a fight? Savitri was all smiles talking to the fellow. Had she ever been so cheerful with him? A wild turmoil stirred up within him. The duo noticed him. Savitri scampered into the house and the fellow jumped onto his rickshaw and sped away. Their parting on seeing him — yes, it clearly suggested something fraudulent, deceitful and intriguing. Savitri was cheating on him all these days, there was no doubt about it. His heart, which had been simmering since morning, was now on fire. He rushed into the house, as if pursued and said, facing Savitri, 'What were you taking to him?'

'What's there to talk to? Nothing.' The same recklessness, the same pride and conceit in her voice.

'I won't have your arrogance today. Answer my question,' he shouted.

'Why do you shout like a drunkard?'

'Yes, I drank today. How does it feel to have a drunkard for your husband?' he yelled and stretching out a vigorous hand, he slapped her across the face. Before she could understand what was happening he slapped her again. But quickly she pushed him away with all her strength and attempted to escape. She tripped and almost fell down but regained her balance in time. Infuriated by her resistance, Raja Rao became terribly violent. He caught hold of her hair and dragged her across the floor. His nails made deep cuts on her body and blood spurted from the gashes. Her blouse came loose and saree got torn. He was unrelenting. He placed a hand on her throat and pinned her against the wall, slapping her the while on the left cheek, then the right and again on the left, till his anger subsided. Savitri collapsed in a heap. It was then that he could effectively bring himself under control. Contrary to his expectation she was not weeping and wailing like Ramayya's wife. In fact she didn't appear to be conscious at all. He looked into her face. It now showed no feeling of scorn, hatred or pride. Like a deer, which had been hit and wounded by a hunter's bullet, she wore the expression of pity, helplessness and misery. He had longed to see Savitri in such a helpless state and the desire had been fulfilled now. The heaviness and constriction he had felt in his heart for the past many months were now gone.

It was much later that he learnt that Savitri got a sack of charcoal delivered by the rickshaw-walla.

"Teerina Korika"
Trans. D. Kesava Rao

# THE TRANSLATORS

**ALLADI UMA** and **M. SRIDHAR** are Reader and Senior Lecturer in English respectively at the University of Hyderabad. Their most recent translation is *The Woman Unbound* (selected short stories) by Volga, a well-known Telugu feminist writer.

**D. KESAVA RAO** is a widely published translator based at Hindupur in Andhra Pradesh. He has translated hundreds of poems and short stories from Telugu. His translation of G.V. Krishna Rao's novel *Puppets* has been brought out by Macmillan recently.

**C.L.L. JAYAPRADA** teaches English at Andhra University, Visakhapatnam. She is well known for her translation of fiction from Telugu. Her translation of Dr. Kesava Reddy's novel *He Conquered the Jungle* has been published by Macmillan.

**P. SHIV KUMAR** teaches English at Kakatiya University, Warangal. He is a distinguished scholar and literary critic. He and Naveen have been close friends since their college days.

**E. SATYANARAYANA** is in the AP Education Service. He has a Ph.D. on Mahasweta Devi. He has more than a dozen published articles to his credit.

**D.V. RAMANI** is the Principal of a college in Hyderabad. Besides an M.A. in English and PGDTE from CIEFL, she has a Post Graduate Diploma in Translation Studies (PGDTS) from the University of Hyderabad.

**V. RADHIKA RANI** is a young scholar and journalist working for the *Indian Express* in Hyderabad.

**B. SHARMILA** has an M.A. from Kakatiya University and PGDTE from CIEFL, Hyderabad. She is keenly interested in translation and language studies.

**NAVEEN** is the author of this book.

**M. RAJESHWAR** is the editor of this book. He teaches English at Kakatiya University, Warangal, Andhra Pradesh. He is the author of *The Novels of Wole Soyinka* and *Indian Women Novelists and Psychoanalysis* and editor of *Postmodernism and English Literature* and *Indian Fiction in English*. His translations of Telugu poetry and short stories have appeared in Sahitya Akademi's journal *Indian Literature* and various anthologies.